Wicked Spell

Dark Spell Series #2

Michelle Escamilla

Wicked Spell

Limitless Publishing, LLC
Kailua, HI 96734
www.limitlesspublishing.com

Formatting: Limitless Publishing

ISBN-13: 978-1-68058-413-4
ISBN-10: 1-68058-413-8

Dedication

I want to dedicate this story to everyone who has helped me push myself and make my stories come to life. Authors, Friends, Readers, Bloggers, and Family. Thank you, everyone.

Chapter One

"What the fuck did you do!" Kyle shouted from the living room. Emma pushed herself from her bed, feeling a little light-headed.

"I swear to God I didn't do anything. She…" Micah began. She could hear the worry in his voice.

"Dude, you need to get the fuck outta my place…" Kyle seethed. Emma walked slowly out of her room and down the hallway to see Kyle and Micah only inches apart. Both of their fists were clenched while staring each other down.

"Will you both back up off each other?" Emma asked, walking into the living room. She grabbed her head as it throbbed. She'd never fainted before, and after this she never wanted to again. Her head was killing her.

"Emma, are you okay?" Kyle asked, rushing to her. She nodded as she stared at Micah. Kyle led her toward the couch to sit down.

"Ky, really, I'm fine. I do need to talk to him though. Mind giving us a sec?" Emma lightly pushed Kyle away.

"Em, I don't know if I trust…"

"Kyle. Please," Emma interrupted. He sighed and nodded before walking toward his room. Once Emma heard the door shut behind him, she turned to Micah. He was taking a seat on the chair across from the couch. "What happened? I don't remember anything," Emma quietly said.

Micah looked down at the floor and let out a sigh. "You were on the phone with your…I mean him, and you threw the phone across the room before you fell to the ground. What did he say?"

"He told me I was going to die and then started spouting off some words, they were unrecognizable, and I don't remember anything else. How did I end up in my bed?"

"I put you in there. I really was worried about you," Micah said before he stood up and sat down next to her. Emma really wanted to get up and leave, but she also wanted to know more from Micah.

"Did you know he wanted to kill me?" she bluntly asked.

"No!" he shouted. "Look, I met him while I was working at my night club. He came in and right away I sensed his powers. He told me he had a business proposition for me. I told him I was actually really busy, but he informed me that it would be worth my time."

"So my dad is pimping me out to random strangers?"

"Emma, it's not like that at all. He told me he would pay quite a bit of money to find his daughter, who he said was really powerful. He gave me the night to think about it, but I'm pretty sure that he used some of his powers to persuade me."

"Once you found out, you didn't think that it was maybe something shady?" she snapped.

"I really just thought that I was finding you for him! I didn't think he was going to do any sort of killing."

"Micah…you said it yourself, you're dark. I'm sure you sensed that my dad was dark! So you think that he's just looking for a family reunion?" The more Emma continued to talk to Micah, the more furious she was becoming with him.

"Emma, you have it all wrong!"

"Do I?" Emma stood up from the couch and crossed her arms. Turning back to face him, it pained her to push him away, but she couldn't be near him anymore. "Micah, I think you should leave," she whispered.

"Emma, when I told you I believed in previous lives, I wasn't kidding. I feel like there is something more to us and I really want to protect you."

"I don't want you to help me. You were helping someone…" Emma started.

"I'm sorry!" he shouted.

Tears began to sting her eyelids and it felt like her heart was breaking into millions of pieces. She wanted so badly to believe him, but she didn't know how she was going to be able to trust him. "Micah, please, I think you should go."

He stood up without another word and walked to the front door. Once the door slammed behind him, the tears finally began to stream down her cheeks.

"Em, you okay?" Kyle asked quietly, startling

Emma. He must've come out of his room after the front door shut.

"Y-yeah," she sobbed.

"Liar. What happened?" Kyle pressed.

"I told him to leave." The more she cried, the worse she felt. She quickly wiped her eyes and sat down on the love seat.

"Uh…isn't that what you wanted?" Kyle took a seat next to her, wrapping his arm around her.

"I guess." It was what she wanted, right?

"Things will get better, Em," Kyle reassured her. "How are you feeling?"

"Besides confused, I'm fine. A bit of a headache," Emma lied. It was worse than a 'bit.' Her head felt like it was going to explode. This was something more than just from fainting.

"Micah said you hit your head on the floor. So, I wouldn't doubt that you fucked up that melon," Kyle joked.

"Shut your face!" She chuckled, grabbing her head.

"Can I get you anything?" he asked her concernedly.

"No, I'm gonna grab some Advil and some water and head to bed."

"It's Friday! Pizza?"

"You know, that actually would be great. I didn't eat when I was out with Damon." Damon's crazed look popped in her head. She was going to have to face him on Monday, something she was not looking forward to.

"Wait, why not? I thought you two were really hitting it off! Well, that's what he was saying at least."

"Yeah, until he tried to force himself on me in the middle of the fucking bar!" Emma snapped. She really didn't want it to come out that way, she originally just wanted to let Kyle down easily—tell him they didn't really hit it off, or something along those lines.

"He *what*?" Kyle seethed.

"Yeah, he said that I owed it to him! Micah…well, he actually helped me out. I was leaving and Damon came after me."

"Jesus! Damon and I are gonna have a little talk on Monday." Kyle made a fist and hit it into his other hand's palm.

"No, don't. I don't think he's even gonna remember," Emma informed him.

"What makes you think that?"

"Kyle. We have magic, remember?" She winked.

"This shit's crazy. How about we come back to reality and order some pizza and chill for the night."

"I'm down for that. You buying?" Emma laughed, walking toward the kitchen. She grabbed a glass from the cupboard and filled it with water. She decided to use her powers to bring the bottle of pills to her. It took a little longer than usual, but it finally began to slide toward her. A sharp pain rushed through her head and down her side afterward. She groaned at the pain.

"Emma?" Kyle hollered as he ran toward her.

"I'm fine. It's just my head." Emma leaned up against the counter, taking a deep breath.

Kyle opened the bottle of medicine and handed her a few capsules along with the water. "Take this, go lie down, and I'll come get you when dinner gets here." He watched her down the pills and chug the water.

"Thanks," she whispered before walking toward her bedroom. A sharp pain in her stomach caused her to pause once she reached the bed. She had felt this pain before, but this time it wasn't as strong as the last time. Once the pain subsided, she lay down on her bed, but didn't bother to take off her clothes. She was only going to rest until the pizza arrived. Emma closed her eyes and rested her arm across them, hoping the throbbing in her head would soon disappear.

***

"Hello, Emma," he said coldly.

"Sebastian," Emma replied.

"Is that any way to speak to your father?"

"Is telling me that you want me dead any way to talk to your child?" she retorted, staring into his eyes.

He sat back into the leather chair. A devilish smile spread across his face. "You look just like your mother when she was your age."

"What do you want from me?" Emma sighed. She knew this wasn't real, it was only a dream. She looked around at a black painted room with only a single lamp and two chairs.

"Plain and simple, I can't have you more powerful than me. I've tried to save you from having to give up your life and work a spell to just take your powers, but that isn't much of an option

now. So, you've got to go."

"I'm not going to let you kill me. If you even come close to me, I will kill you myself," Emma threatened.

"Wow, feeling a little powerful? You don't know what you're getting yourself into, young lady. Do you know what I can do?"

"No, but I'm sure willing to find out. Get out of my fucking head!" Emma grabbed her head and ducked down into a ball. She rocked back and forth to get him away from her.

***

"Emma, will you please wake up?" Kyle rubbed her arm.

"Hmm?" Emma's eyes began to flutter open. She could see Kyle sitting on her bed, looking exhausted. He looked different, almost as if he grew loads of facial stubble in the last hour.

"I tried to wake you up a few times, but I couldn't get you to even make a sound."

"Is pizza here?" Emma asked, stretching.

"Em, it's Sunday morning!" Kyle exclaimed.

She quickly sat up. "What?"

"I've never been so worried about you! Karen came over and we took turns just waiting for you to make some movement. I almost called the coroner at one point. Dude, you looked fucking dead, but you had a pulse and were still breathing."

"Well, thanks for not calling them to take me away in a body bag." Emma chuckled—she could only joke about the situation. She had no idea how she slept that long.

"I'm serious though…" He looked down at the floor.

"What?" she asked.

"I called…I called your mom and she's on her way out here."

"You did what?" Emma shouted, pushing herself out of bed. Her head felt a little foggy, but the massive throbbing pain she had finally died down.

"You were out and I had no idea what to do. I didn't really want to involve a doctor 'cause then they probably would've involved the police. I was even about to call Micah, but hey, on the bright side, I didn't."

"Great, do you want some sort of reward?" Emma sarcastically asked Kyle.

"Uh, no, but maybe a 'thanks, Kyle, for trying to take care of me,' that would be great!"

"You're right, thanks to you and Karen for watching out for me. But why'd you call my mom?" Emma whined. She only knew that her mom would worry and want to take her somewhere far away from all of this. Granted, Emma needed to be as far away from Sebastian as possible, but she couldn't run forever.

"She was the only person who could help you out. I know this is something outside of the 'normal' people kind of thing. It was her or Micah, so take your pick."

"Shit," she whispered. "When will she be here?"

"Karen actually went to pick her up."

"You sent your girlfriend to pick her up?" Emma asked, walking toward her bathroom. She was still wearing her shirt from Friday, but she noticed that she wasn't wearing any pants. "Where are my jeans?" Emma laughed, pointing to her bare legs.

"Well, I…" Kyle blushed.

"Taking advantage of someone who is unconscious? That's kinda below you, is it not?"

"You're such a dick. I wanted to make sure you were comfortable while you were in your coma. Sue me."

"Thanks for helping me. I mean it." Emma walked into her bathroom and brushed her teeth. Staring at herself in the mirror, she began to think of what could have possibly happened that made her pass out for that long. There were black rings under her eyes. She looked like she was back from the dead. She peeked out of the bathroom and noticed Kyle had left her room.

Emma slipped on some of her lounge pants and searched her room for her phone. As she dug through her bag, she could hear Kyle on the phone with someone. "Yeah, she's up. I don't know, she won't tell me. Well, just as soon as you can. All right, see ya."

She felt a rush of power begin to overwhelm her. She tried to push the feeling aside but it only made it worse. She began to see everything in tunnel vision and so she closed her eyes. Suddenly, her lamp shattered. "Oh shit," Emma breathed, getting back into her bed.

"What the fuck, Em?" Kyle ran into the room.

"I…I don't know. I heard you talking to someone and I got this…the lamp broke."

"You got what? Karen called, she was telling me

she's on her way back. Your mom got on the line and I was talking to her!"

"I'm…there's definitely something wrong. How long until they get here?" Emma asked shakily.

"Thirty minutes. Why don't you lay your crazy ass down and I'll grab you something to drink."

"Coffee, please," Emma requested as she lay on her pillow. She really did need her mom here—all this shit was going to drive her nuts. Emma began to wonder if she should call Micah; he could help her understand her dad a little more. She tried to rid that idea from her head. As she was tying her hair into a ponytail, Kyle came back into her room with a mug of coffee. "Thank you. And you put cream in it? You're so sweet!"

Kyle smiled as he sat down on the edge of her bed. "Wanna tell me what's really going on? I hate being in the dark, Em. I know about your 'powers,' so maybe I can help you."

"Kyle, I'd love to tell you what the hell is going on. I just don't know what the hell is going on! Daddy Dearest called me and one minute he's saying I'm going to die and the next he's mumbling something and I'm seeing shit in tunnel vision."

"Oh…I'm actually, for once, at a total loss for words."

"Shit, someone write it down. Quick!" Emma joked, pretending to look for a pen in her nightstand.

"Very funny, smart-ass. Drink your coffee. I'm gonna clean up the lamp you decided to break before your mom gets here. Oh, is she still single?"

"Gross, dude. That's my mom! And she's

actually seeing a guy."

"Lucky bastard." Kyle chuckled, leaving the room. Emma snuggled into her comforter and sipped on the hot coffee. Her phone vibrated on the end table.

Leaning over, Emma answered the call, "Hello?"

"How are you feeling?" Micah said.

"A little out of it. What's up?"

"I wanted to make sure that you're okay. Can I help with anything?" Micah asked solemnly.

"Micah, I think that you've done more than enough…" she started.

"Emma, I don't know how I can prove to you that I'm sorry."

"How about leaving me alone?"

"Don't worry. I'm heading back to New York next weekend."

"For good?" Her voice hitched.

"Yeah, I'm going to work out of my club out there. I just wanted to make sure you were okay before I left."

"I-I'm…I'm fine." Emma suddenly didn't want him to leave. She knew he'd betrayed her, but…"All right. Well…"

"Goodbye, Emma."

"Bye," she sobbed. And he hung up. She wished her mom would get there sooner.

Chapter Two

After spending twenty minutes in the bathroom, bawling her eyes out, Emma finally made her way out to hear her mom in the living room. Emma hurried toward her mom, where she greeted Emma with arms wide open. "Hi, Mom!" Emma said, squeezing her mom tightly.

"Hi, sweetheart. How are you doing?"

"I'm…I'm good." Emma turned to Karen. "Thank you for picking her up."

"Oh, it's no problem," Karen said cheerfully.

"Grace, it's so nice to see you again," Kyle greeted Emma's mom, hugging her.

"Kyle, that better be your keys poking my leg," her mom joked.

"Nope, all me," he laughed.

The look on Karen's face made it obvious that she had yet to be informed of the brother-sister relationship that they had, or of the ongoing joke of Kyle being in love with Emma's mom. "Sorry, Kar. It's a joke," he reassured her, pulling her into his side.

Karen let out a sigh of relief. "Do you think we should give them some time alone?" she asked, pushing him toward the front door.

"Yeah, let's go get some food. Do you guys want anything?" he asked, grabbing his jacket.

"No, I'm fine. Mom?"

"No, I ate before my flight. Connor had a wonderful breakfast made for me." She was glowing at the mention of Connor's name.

Emma waved to Karen and Kyle as they headed out the door. "Mom, can I get you something to drink at least?" Emma asked as she locked the door, then walked toward the kitchen.

"No, I'm fine, thank you. Why don't you come tell me what happened," she insisted, patting the couch cushion next to her as she took a seat. Sitting down next to her, Emma began to fidget with her fingers. "So?"

"Well, Micah was working for my dad. Micah said that he was sent only to find me, that dad has been trying to find me." Emma's legs began to bounce up and down.

"Okay, I know that much." She placed her hand on Emma's lap to calm her.

"Micah, he saved me from a guy I thought was good. He brought me home and then he answered a phone call…it turned out to be my dad. He wanted to talk to me…." Tears began to stream down her cheeks as she recalled the conversation. "He wants me to die!"

"Emma, I won't let anything happen to you. Oh, sweetie, don't cry," she said, wiping the tears away.

"Mom, what can you do? He's gonna try

everything and you've hidden me my entire life from him, but he's found me now. I can't live in hiding."

"No, you can't. I can do my best to help you get stronger. I know we practiced when you were with me during Christmas, but now we really have to get you more powerful."

"How long are you here for?" Emma asked, grabbing a tissue off the coffee table.

"As long as you need me."

"What about the store? What about Connor?"

"The bookstore isn't a worry. I have a friend who will manage it for me. As for Connor, he understands that you're in trouble, so he's not going anywhere."

"Does he know?"

"No. Not yet. I don't want to scare him away; we've only been together for a short time."

"Why can't I have a 'normal' relationship?" Emma chuckled.

"'Cause you're special and you don't want anything ordinary. You never have." She smiled as she stood up. "Can I set my things in your room?"

"Oh, you can have my room! I'll sleep out here on the couch!"

"Honey, I don't want you to give up your room," her mom insisted.

"Seriously, it's okay. I'll help you carry your bag." Emma walked over to her mom's suitcase. "Did you only bring this *one* bag?"

"Some of us don't need four bags to travel." Grace laughed. Emma rolled her eyes as she picked up the bag and carried it down the hall to her room.

It was so nice to have her mom here. "Okay, tell me the rest of what happened," she said, following Emma to her room.

"I *wish* I knew. What I remember is…Micah came over, he had to talk to me, but before he could even start, his phone rang. He told me it was for me. I answered and it was my dad. After he told me that I was going to die, he started spouting off some words, but I couldn't understand what he was saying…" Emma sat down on the bed, trying to remember at least one of the words that he used. "I can't even remember one phrase. Micah said I tossed his phone and fainted."

"I don't know any spells over the phone, but then again I only know spells that help people. I don't know how much help I'm going to be for that." Emma's mom began to inspect the room, checking for dust and cleanliness.

"I figured. Kyle said that he called you 'cause I wouldn't wake up. Would that have anything to do with it?"

"Sweetie, I don't know if that was part of it, but it could've been. He was really worried about you. Have you been around any strange people who could have given you something?"

"I went out with a co-worker, but I left before I could eat or drink anything, and Micah was there to pick me up. He's the only one, but I doubt he'd do anything…well, more."

"Have you noticed anything weird happening to you?"

"Mom, I just recently found out I'm a witch! Yeah, everything that happens to me is weird."

Her mom chuckled. "I meant other than that."

"Actually, every once in a while I get a sharp pain in my abdomen. It causes me to stop what I'm doing and hurts for a few minutes and then goes away."

"How long has it been doing that?" she asked, sitting down beside Emma.

"Right after I met Micah." Emma sighed. She tried to recall if it had happened any time before Micah, but no time came to mind.

"I really think that is your way of 'sensing' dark magic around you."

"But I never got it around Micah."

"I hate to say it, but maybe Micah isn't as dark as he thinks he is."

Emma's head started to lightly throb again. Micah continuously said that he went dark, but was he just saying that under the orders of her dad? "So you think it was my dad getting me to go dark through Micah?"

Her mom nodded. "It's a possibility. If your dad is around, or near you, you're maybe sensing him."

"He said that he'd been watching me. But the pain is touch and go."

"Emma, so are your powers. Maybe as you get stronger and more used to the idea of using your powers on a daily basis the pain will become more consistent."

Emma leaned back onto the mattress, pulling the pillow over her face, growling into it. Her mom slapped her leg and she removed the pillow off of her face. "Mom, everything seems so crazy. I need this to all go away."

"I know, sweetie. I'm so sorry this is going on. If I could change it, I would."

"Maybe I could get Micah to do his 'eraser' thingy on my dad and make him forget all about me." Emma laughed. Her mom cracked a smile.

"Sorry, I wish it was that easy. Micah might have powers, but he has nothing on you or your father."

"So, do you think that my father is stronger than me?"

"Let's get you some tea…" her mom began.

"Mom?"

"He could be. If he had the right help or the right practice, then yes, he could be stronger than when we were married."

"Ah shit." Emma felt a sinking feeling in her stomach.

"Emma, don't swear," her mom scolded.

"I think I need something stronger than tea. Want a beer?"

"A beer would be nice."

They headed into the kitchen, and Grace took a seat at the table while Emma opened two beers. They sat in silence, drinking their beers. Emma couldn't help but think about if she was going to have to face her father and what was actually going to happen. She was going to ask her mom for a plan of attack when Kyle and Karen walked in through the door.

"Hey, guys," Emma said, lifting her beer up.

"I know you guys said you weren't hungry, but we brought Chinese and alcohol," Kyle said, cheerily holding up a paper bag filled with Chinese containers while Karen held up two bottles of wine. Emma smiled widely at Karen as she handed Emma the bottles. Kyle grabbed four plates out of the cabinet and placed them on the counter. Emma poured four glasses of wine.

"Grace, what can I get you?" Kyle asked, scooping some Lo Mein onto a plate.

"Thanks, but I'm still fine. I will take a glass of that wine though." Grace smiled.

"My kinda lady," Kyle joked. Emma and Karen both smacked Kyle's arm. "Ow! What?"

"Quit hitting on my mom!" Emma laughed.

"Em, your mom is hot! I'm just telling the truth."

"Thanks, Kyle. I appreciate it," Grace chimed in. "It's good to know that I still got it."

Emma filled her plate with chicken fried rice and crab and cheese wontons. "Karen, what can I get you?" Emma asked, taking a bite of the wonton.

"Oh, don't worry about mine, I'll get it. Here's your glass, though," Karen responded, giving Emma a glass of wine.

The four of them sat around the table, talking about everything from family memories to favorite places to visit. Grace called it an early night and headed into the bedroom, closing the door. Emma, Karen, and Kyle decided to move from wine to shots of the rum that was in the freezer. They thought it would be a good idea to play board games and watch movies in Spanish. Emma was forever grateful that she had Kyle, and now Karen, in her life.

Chapter Three

"Good morning, sleepy head," Grace said quietly, rubbing Emma's head.

She cracked one of her eyes open to see her mom sitting next to her on the couch. "What time is it?" Emma asked hoarsely.

"Nine. I was thinking we could get some coffee and find a park to start practicing."

"Ugh," Emma grunted, rolling over. She tried to cover her head with the blanket, but her mom pulled it down.

"Get up. I'm serious."

"You're too cheery in the morning," Emma snapped, pulling the covers back from her mom. Without a second thought, she used her powers to lift her mom off the couch and move her to the love seat next to her.

Her mom gasped. "Emma Morgan!"

"What?"

"Do you realize what you just did?"

"I was just asleep. What do you mean what I just did?" Emma yawned, sitting up.

"What do you mean you were just asleep?" her mom asked, puzzled. "I was just having a conversation with you about going to get coffee and starting to work on your powers."

"Mom, I swear I was just asleep!" Emma realized only then that mixing wine with hard liquor was a horrible idea. "And I'm seriously feeling like crap, but I'd love to get some coffee."

Grace pushed herself up from the couch and walked back over to Emma and sat beside her. "I think we have a problem," she said worriedly.

"What kind of problem?" Emma began to feel her heart race.

"I think whatever your dad said to you over the phone was something bad, and…"

"Mom?"

"Honey, I'm not that educated in darker magic. It was something I had no desire in learning, so I have no idea what to do to reverse this."

Emma dropped her head. "I know a couple of people." She knew that she was going to have to bring Micah and Ying in on this. She wasn't keen on the idea, but knew they were the only two people, besides her dad, who knew dark magic and could help her.

Grace knew who Emma was thinking of. She nodded her head and stood up. "Well, go get ready and we'll go." Grace sighed. Emma nodded as she slowly pushed herself off the couch.

Emma made her way into her bathroom to get showered. She was not looking forward to asking Micah for help. Things were definitely unresolved between the two of them, and for her to go back to him to get help was not something she was happy about. As she waited for the water to warm up, the sharp pain in her side caused her to double over. Looking in the mirror, she thought she saw the image of a man standing behind her. She grabbed the counter before she fell over.

"Mom!" she called out as tears began to stream down her cheeks.

"Emma? What's the matter?" He mom came running into the bathroom. She helped her up, assisting her to the bed.

"I...I don't know. I was waiting for the wat...this hurts," Emma whispered, lying down on the bed.

"Well, just rest for a moment. I'm going to see if I can take away some of the pain." Grace began to whisper as she placed her hands on Emma's stomach, where she had been clenching. Emma felt the pain slowly disappearing. "How are you feeling?"

Emma sighed. "A little better, thank you. I was waiting for the water to warm up and I could've sworn I saw a guy standing behind me. He had an evil smile on his face. He looked just so...he looked like this guy I ran into not too long ago..." Emma paused.

"What did he look like?" Grace asked anxiously.

"Salt and pepper hair, possibly some facial hair? Blue eyes for sure, they were very cold. Good looking, but something really dark about him."

"That was your dad."

"Mom, are you sure? It's been years since you saw him."

"I just have a feeling. The cold blue eyes give it away. Even if it isn't, don't you find it a little strange that you'd think about some random man that you ran into on the street?"

"You're right. All right, I need to get in the shower. The quicker we talk to Ying and Micah, the quicker I can get back to life."

Her mom nodded, helping Emma off the bed. Grace left the room and Emma walked back toward the bathroom. She was rather skeptical to look into the mirror, but wanted to make sure she didn't see another image of him standing there. Nothing. The water was still running. This time it was warm as she ran her fingers underneath the faucet. Emma quickly undressed and stepped into the tub.

***

After Emma finished getting ready, she called a taxi while she waited for her mom. She was going to call Micah to come and pick her up, but figured it was best for him to meet her down at Ying's shop. She sent him a quick text message.

Hi. I need the address for Ying's shop. If you could also meet me there, I'd appreciate it.

"Are you ready?" Grace asked, wrapping a scarf around her neck.

"Yeah, taxi should be here in about five. I just sent Micah a text, telling him I need to meet him."

"I know this is going to be hard, but he might help. I know you aren't thrilled about it; believe me,

22

I'm not excited to ask for help from a guy who was going have my daughter harmed, but let's just see what he has to say."

Emma's phone vibrated.

Micah: It's in the Highlands. Can't miss it. I'll be there in 20.

"He'll be there in twenty. My stomach is in knots." Emma grabbed her purse and walked toward the front door. "Well, let's go. This has already been an interesting morning, why stop the party now."

As they walked out of the building, a taxi was waiting for them at the curb. Emma told the driver to just head toward the Highlands area, but didn't have the exact address. He didn't seem too pleased to hear that she didn't have the address, but sped off. Emma and her mom sat in silence the entire drive. Monday traffic seemed quite light for it being rush hour. Emma pulled out her cell phone and gave Kyle a call.

"Hello?" he answered quietly.

"Hey, you at work?" Emma asked, checking the time.

"Yeah, Phil is showing some new people around so I didn't want them to see me on my cell. I'm in the breakroom now, what's up?"

"I didn't hear you leave this morning, so I just wanted to make sure you were there. Wait, new people? He's not replacing me, is he?"

"No! He had to get a replacement for Damon. Apparently, he called Phil over the weekend and told him that he needed to change his life around or some Ricki Lake bullshit and hung up on him. Phil has been kinda pissy today."

"Damon quit?"

"Yeah," Kyle replied with a chuckle.

Emma began to wonder if Micah had something to do with it. Grace peeked over at Emma and she held a finger up to her. "Well, hey, I'll be back at work tomorrow."

"Take the week off. We're fine. There's a new girl who will be working in accounting, her name is Paula, and she's going to help out while you're gone. Bonus for me too—she's kinda hot."

"Kyle! I'm telling Karen!" Emma laughed.

"I'm just saying she's kinda hot!"

Emma rolled her eyes. "Are you sure I should take this week off? It sounds like you guys are busy."

"Nah, get things fixed," Kyle reassured.

"Ma'am, where are we going from here?" the cab driver interrupted.

"Where are you?" Kyle asked.

"Down the road, like three more blocks. And I'm on my way to visit a…friend with my mom." The cab driver seemed confused as he looked at Emma in the rearview mirror. "Hey, Ky, I gotta go. I'll call you later." Emma hung the phone up and tossed it into her bag.

"Sir, this is the place," Grace said, tapping on the driver's shoulder.

"Thanks, Mom."

The car came to a stop. Emma slipped the guy some cash and slid behind her mom, exiting the car.

Emma looked at the building, remembering the last time she was here. As she walked toward the entrance, Micah's SUV pulled up to the curb. Emma's heart began to race, he looked so good.

"Hey," he greeted Emma as he walked toward her, staring into her eyes.

"Hi. I'm going to need your help." Emma sighed, breaking their stare and looking over to her mom.

"Of course, but why are we at Ying's?"

"You both are going to help me," Emma stated, walking away from Micah and into the shop.

Grace and Emma looked around the shop for Ying, but she was nowhere in sight. Emma turned back toward Micah. "Do you know where she is?"

Micah shook his head as he walked back toward the office. Emma watched him poke his head into the room and look back, shaking his head. Emma began to panic; she couldn't have gone very far with her shop unlocked and her merchandise all available.

"You don't think that…" Grace began.

"That I'd take her and hurt her?" a male asked, walking out from behind a curtain that was off to the side. "Grace, you're still so beautiful."

"Sebastian, what are you doing here?" Grace whispered, pulling Emma toward her. Micah quickly stepped in front of Grace and Emma.

"Oh come on, Micah. I'd never hurt them in the middle of a public place. You should know better than that," Sebastian scolded.

"I'm not taking any chances. I won't let you hurt either one of them, so maybe you should get the fuck outta here, Blackwood."

"Where's Ying?" Emma interrupted.

"She wanted to clear out of here before you all showed up. She thought it would be nice for me to have a special reunion with my daughter. Who knew I'd get my beautiful wife in the process."

"Sebastian, why can't you leave our daughter alone? You don't need her!" Grace said shakily.

"You daft woman. You know exactly why I need her. Don't worry, I'm not going to do anything today. I just wanted to see her."

"Well, you saw me. I'm sorry I couldn't say I missed you or that I'm thrilled to finally see you after all these years, but…"

"Don't talk to me that way, young lady. I could end you right now, but I won't! So, with that being said, I'm sure I'll see you soon."

Emma began to see him in tunnel vision, and the room began to darken. "Emma, calm down," Micah whispered, placing his hand on her lower back. The room began to lighten up. "That's my girl."

Emma gave him a look and took a step away from him.

"I'm sensing that you were trying to use some magic on me," Sebastian said. "Remember, I'm a little more experienced than you. Don't start something that you're not ready to finish," he threatened as he started for the door.

The three of them sighed with heavy relief once Sebastian was out of the building. "Micah, I'm not your girl!" Emma scolded, walking away from Grace and him.

"I…that's not what I meant! Look, how do you

want my help?" Micah crossed his arms, annoyed with Emma for snapping at him.

"Emma is going to need some help understanding the way Sebastian works. I'm going to help her as much as I can with her powers," Grace chimed in.

Micah nodded. "How was Ying going to help?"

"She's the only other person who knows Sebastian. I wanted her to help Emma. She…"

"She really can't do much magic anymore. Sebastian tried to experiment on her, basically preparing for the day he met Emma. He ruined her," Micah said solemnly.

Emma looked at Micah in shock. She thought Ying's powers had diminished in other ways—she didn't realize that her father was responsible for weakening her. "I thought she could sense I was stronger?" Emma asked.

"She can just sense magic now, but she used to be able to do so much more," Micah answered, uncrossing his arms.

"Oh," Emma said quietly.

"Well, Micah…where do we begin?" Grace asked, leaning against a table.

"Let's head back to my place…"

"For what?" Emma interrupted.

"I've got lots of space—all of my stuff is pretty much moved out and we can use the openness to get some practice."

"I forgot," Emma whispered.

"Are you leaving, Micah?" Grace asked, walking toward Emma.

"Yeah, I'm heading back to New York. I…"

"Let's head to your place." Emma stopped him. "Can we ride with you?"

"Of course."

They walked out of the shop and got into Micah's SUV. Emma needed to work on her powers and take her mind off of Micah leaving.

Chapter Four

The entire drive was silent. Once they arrived, Emma followed her mom and Micah into his loft, feeling a little nervous to be back in his place. It felt like it was so long ago, yet it was only weeks. As she walked in, she noticed that most of his place was empty—it didn't even feel like his place anymore.

"So you're really moving?" Emma asked.

"Yeah," he replied quietly. "Grace, can I get you anything? Emma?"

Grace shook her head, but Emma nodded. "I'll have some water, please. When are you leaving?"

"Soon. We should probably get started and then we can order some dinner whenever you get hungry," he stated, placing a water-filled glass in front of Emma. She continued to look only at him. Had they not broken up, would he be leaving now? She wanted to press the matter, but with her mom being there, she didn't want to get into it.

"Emma?" Grace whispered.

"I'm fine. I…let's get to work. What do we need

to do?" Emma asked solemnly.

"Micah, you've tried to teach Emma dark magic. How much did you learn from Sebastian, if any?" Grace asked, setting her coat on a chair.

"I didn't learn anything from him. I had some friends back east that practiced a bit, but they didn't know a lot about it. Since I was the only one with actual powers, I started to train a bit more. Ying helped me a little bit."

"So, you were encouraging her to learn dark for Sebastian?" Grace questioned him, taking a seat on the couch.

"Correct. I enjoy the dark aspect of witchcraft, but I'm hardly fully dark." Micah avoided eye contact with Emma. Almost as if he was embarrassed by the omission.

Emma didn't want to say anything. She sat down on the couch next to her mom and kept her eyes on the floor. Yet another lie from Micah's mouth.

"Emma, I'm going to have you practice with Micah on what he knows. I'm going to get you better at healing and anything else I can. I think that healing is going to be really important in this situation," Grace said, standing up. "Micah, I'm going to need you to teach her everything that you know. I'm also going to make some phone calls to see if I can get someone to reverse the spell that was placed on Emma when she was a child."

"What spell did you put on her?" Micah inquired.

"I had a friend of mine take away the memory of her having powers. If that can come off, she's going to be really strong, really fast. As a kid, she could do some pretty amazing things. I think that's when her dad was getting really obsessed with taking her powers."

"I'm so glad that you two are having a conversation about me and not with me!" Emma snapped. She quickly stood up and began to levitate the couch.

"Emma!" Micah shouted. "How long has she been randomly snapping like this?" he asked Grace.

"This morning was the first I'd seen. It was like she was awake, but wasn't!" Grace panicked.

Micah waved his hands at the couch, bringing it back to the ground, and then used his powers to sit Emma down. "Emma, snap out of it!"

"What are you doing?" Emma asked, confused.

"You were in a dark moment, you had the couch up over your head," Micah informed her.

"What is going on?" Emma began to tear up. "First my mom said I was doing something this morning and I don't remember, and now this!"

"I'm sure that your dad put a spell on you that night over the phone. I'm going to try and take it off, but..."

"But what?" Emma wiped the tears from her cheek.

"I'm not an expert, so you're going to have to be patient with me." Micah placed his hand on Emma's lap.

"What are you going to do? Make me blind or something?"

Micah chuckled. "No, nothing like that. It's a potion from the bar. It just might make you feel a little sick, but that is if it works correctly. If I don't get it right, you won't feel anything."

"Isn't that usually the other way around?" Emma asked, trying not to smile.

"You'd think so, but you're going to want to get rid of whatever is taking over you. Like a virus, you want it out of your body."

Emma nodded as Micah pulled her into a hug. She took a deep breath in, smelling his cologne. She now didn't want him to leave.

Grace cleared her throat, breaking them apart. "Micah can you make that potion? I'm going to start working with her on the healing."

"Sure, I'll have to run down to the club and make it. You can help yourself to whatever is in the fridge and I'll be back in about thirty."

Grace nodded and Emma walked him to the door. "Be careful," Emma whispered. Micah smiled as he headed out and Emma locked the door behind him. She turned to face her mom, who was giving her a look. "What?" Emma asked.

"Nothing. Well, I just see how you are with him. I think that you want him to stay."

"Don't be ridiculous. He's ruined his chance," Emma scoffed. She walked back toward the couch.

"You know, I'm not that old." Grace chuckled. "I know that look you gave him when he left. I know that extra-long embrace."

"Okay, well, he's leaving and I can't stop him."

"I'm sure you could, but right now you don't want to. I get it."

"Mom, are you on his side now?" Emma crossed her arms.

"I didn't say that. Emma, he wants to help you,

and if he really wanted to hurt you, I'm sure he could have. Maybe he's not that bad after all."

"I really don't want to talk about this right now!" Emma plopped down on the couch, rubbing her temples.

"Fine. We'll get to work, then." Grace walked toward Emma, whispering something under her breath.

"What are you doing?" Emma screeched, standing up. She could feel the room getting colder. Suddenly Emma's fingers felt numb, almost as if she was getting frost bite.

"Paper cuts can be easy, but when you've had a spell to make things happen to your body—it's not as simple. So, I want you to try to heal your fingers even though you can't move them."

Emma tried to move her hands, but the more she moved them, the more they hurt. "I…I can't!"

"Remember that you don't need your hands. Your powers are within your whole body. You can use your mind, your eyes."

Emma began to concentrate on both of her hands, trying to put her power into making her finger move again. Her fingers started to feel like they were underneath a heater, like they were defrosting. Her pinkie finger began to twitch. "I'm doing it!" Emma shouted excitedly. She tried to focus a little harder to get the rest of her fingers to move.

"I'm very proud of you, Emma. You did really well. I didn't even have to step in and help."

"Thank you, Mom," Emma said, smiling. She was pretty proud of herself too. "I'm kinda hungry.

Should we fix some breakfast and have it ready when he gets back?"

Grace smiled. "That'd be nice. Does he have stuff to make it?"

Emma ran over to the fridge to find a gallon of orange juice, leftover Chinese boxes, and a jar of pickles. She shut the door, disgusted, and huffed. "He's got orange juice, I'll give him that." Emma laughed. "I'm going to call this diner that is down the road—they deliver." Emma grabbed her phone out of her purse and searched for the number for the diner. Once she found the place, she called them and ordered a variety of breakfast items. They gave her a total and told her they'd be there in twenty minutes.

***

Emma and her mom practiced a few more times on Emma's healing powers. Emma felt she was getting better each time. Emma checked the time— she was getting nervous that Micah had yet to return. The food arrived a few minutes late, but she was too hungry to argue. Grace went to the kitchen to grab some dishware and found all the cabinets had been cleaned out.

"They gave us silverware!" Emma exclaimed as she heard her mom slamming cabinet doors.

"Seriously? What is he eating with?" Grace scoffed.

"I've been eating at the bar, mostly," Micah answered, walking in through the front door.

"What took you so long?" Emma asked,

checking her phone. He had been gone closer to an hour.

"Sorry, I was trying to make sure I had everything, and since it's been forever since I made this, I had to wait for it."

"Who'd you have to use this on?" Grace asked, pulling the tops off the Styrofoam boxes to use them as plates. She began to divide the eggs and pancakes among the three of them.

"My mom," Micah answered quietly.

"Your mom? Why?" Emma asked, surprised.

"My mom got into some trouble with some other people. I had to make sure that she was okay, so she taught me how to do it. I just hope that it works."

Emma started to take a bite of a pancake when Micah pulled the fork away from her. "Hey! I was eating that!"

"I know, but if this drink works… it's gonna make it all come up—let's do this first and then you can eat," Micah stated, taking a bite of her pancakes. Emma shot him a dirty look. He quickly shook the drink in the martini shaker and opened it up. "It smells, well, horrible. It's best that you just down it."

Emma cringed as she brought the cup up to her lips. She quickly downed the liquid. It had the consistency of a milkshake, but the taste of someone's gym socks. Emma gagged as she swallowed the last few drops. "How long does it take?" Emma asked, but before anyone could answer, she began to feel nauseous. She ran across the loft toward the bathroom, trying not to fall over.

"I guess you didn't forget how to make it,"

Grace sarcastically said, walking toward the bathroom. "Emma? You okay?" she asked, knocking on the door. She could hear Emma vomiting, so she turned around and walked back toward Micah.

"Is she throwing up?" he asked, taking a bite of eggs.

Grace nodded. "Yeah. Are you sure it's working, or could it be just the taste of it?"

"Oh my God!" Emma shrieked. Micah ran toward the bathroom and opened the door. Emma pushed herself away from the toilet. "What the fuck is that?"

Micah peeked into the toilet and saw what resembled a newt. "It worked. How do you feel?"

"Like, I'm going to have nightmares about puking up a lizard!" She quickly flushed the toilet to rid the image.

"You'll forget about it. Besides, it wasn't real, just part of the spell. Unless something else was cast, you should start to feel better. Wanna come eat?"

"I think I lost my appetite," Emma sulked as she followed Micah out of the bathroom. Emma took a deep breath and noticed she did feel a bit better. She hesitantly took a bite of her pancakes and realized that she wasn't going to be sick from her food. She began to eat with everyone.

"Emma, I'm going to work with you a bit more on what we had done before. I think you could use a little more practice. I also think that, and I'm hoping your mom will agree with me, you should work on using multiple powers at the same time." Micah looked over at Grace, who was nodding in agreement.

"Don't you think I should learn them separately first?" Emma asked, pushing the makeshift plate away.

"We don't know how long Sebastian is going to be generous," Micah stated. "I don't know if he's up to something, but I'm really shocked that he didn't try anything at La Bella Morte. He tried to play himself off as being nice, but he's up to something."

"Then what are we waiting for?" Emma asked, wiping her hands.

Micah started off right away, lifting Emma into the air. Her mom began to whisper words. Emma felt like the air around her was slipping away from her. She suddenly wished that she had some of that dark spell left in her—she seemed more powerful with it. Emma could see Micah staring at her intently; she tried to channel any and all of their moments and put them into one ball of emotion.

"You can do it," Micah mouthed to Emma. She began to feel her hands cramp, but this time her mom didn't make them cold, they felt broken.

Emma felt like she was going to suffocate. She closed her eyes and imagined herself in an open field. She was able to breathe, it was just in her head. Emma quickly began to heal her fingers, and then quickly sent a wave of power toward Micah, pushing him backwards. He tried to use his powers again, but Emma lifted him up and tossed him onto the bed.

"I think that you're going to be great," Micah

said, pushing himself off the bed.

Emma rubbed her hands—they felt really cramped compared to the last time. "Mom, what did you do to my fingers this time?"

"Sorry, I broke your fingers. Making them cold didn't appear to be a challenge."

"You did what? I can't believe that!" Emma exclaimed in disbelief.

"You healed yourself though!" Grace shrugged, walking toward Emma.

The three of them continued to practice throughout the rest of the afternoon. Grace showed Micah some simple ways to heal, but he didn't have that ability so it didn't work as well. Micah did show them how he had the ability to work with people's minds. Emma wanted to ask him about what was said to Damon, but realized she didn't want to ruin the fun or bring him up.

Micah had ordered them pizza and before they knew it, the time was already eight o'clock. Grace had insisted on calling a cab, but Micah ended up winning the battle and drove them home.

"Micah, thank you so much for helping today," Grace said as they pulled up to Emma's apartment building.

"It was my pleasure, Grace," he replied, smiling at Emma.

"Well, I'm going to head upstairs to bed. Emma, don't be too long."

"I'll be up in just a minute," Emma reassured. Grace exited the SUV and closed the door. Emma turned toward Micah. "When do you leave?"

"Tomorrow night."

"Wow. That's really soon."

"I'm really sorry. About everything," Micah said, holding Emma's hand.

"Micah…" Emma started.

"I know. I hurt you and I really didn't mean to. I never imagined in the entire time that I was working for him I'd fall for you. Emma, I really…look, if you need anything, please call me. I'll be here in a flash for you," Micah stated. Emma nodded, leaning in and hugging him. Micah pressed his lips against her head.

She wanted so much more of him, but knew that it was not a good idea. She pulled away from him. "Goodbye, Micah."

She walked into the building, not looking back at him—she didn't want to show him that she was starting to cry. She walked into her apartment to see Kyle lounging on the couch.

"Hey, Hermione, how was Hogwarts?" Kyle joked.

"You're stupid!" Emma laughed. She could always rely on Kyle for making a shitty situation better. Emma sat down next to him as he flipped through channels.

"Your owl, he actually made a great dinner. And it turns out that one of your professors is in trouble with the law…" he paused, looking around, then whispered "…posed in *Playgirl*."

"Shut up! For the love of everything! Anyway, where's Karen?" Emma asked, looking around.

"She's staying at her place tonight. Her dad is in town so she wanted to spend time with him. I guess he's staying at her place."

"Ah. Well, you're on my bed, and I'm exhausted." Emma kicked off her shoes and grabbed her lounge pants. "I also need some privacy to change."

"No, you really don't." Kyle chuckled.

"Good night, Kyle." Emma laughed, tossing a throw pillow at his head.

"All right, all right! I can tell when I'm not wanted. I'll see ya in the morning."

Emma waved to him as he walked into his bedroom. She quickly changed into her pajamas and lay down on the couch. She had never felt so tired from just practicing magic. Hopefully, if Sebastian tried anything, she'd be ready.

Chapter Five

"Daddy! Look at this beautiful picture I made!"

"Emma, that's great! Daddy has something to show you. Can you come downstairs with me?" Sebastian asked, setting her drawing on the table.

"A surprise!" Emma shouted excitedly, knocking some papers on the floor.

"Yep, come on."

Emma could feel the cold of the basement. As she hit the bottom of the stairs her dad lifted her with powers and placed her on a table. Her heart was racing.

"Daddy! What's going on?" Emma panicked. She tried to use her powers to push him back, but this time she couldn't. He seemed so much stronger than when she started to learn about her powers.

"Emma, hold still. You won't feel anything after this. Just remember that Daddy loves you."

Emma began to cry as the room started to darken around her.

***

"Emma, you okay?" Grace whispered, rubbing Emma's back.

Emma was sobbing into her pillow. "He tried to kill me when I was little. Who would do such a thing?"

"Your father…he's…I'm sorry, honey."

Emma sat up to see that it was light out and her mom's suitcase was next to the chair. "Mom? Are you leaving?"

"Yeah. I think you are a lot stronger than I realized." Her mom smiled. "If you need *anything*, call me right away. I'm sure that if anything comes up and I need to come out here right away, Connor can bring me."

"I don't want you to leave yet," Emma sobbed.

"I know. I love being able to spend time with you. Let's not wait another year, okay?"

Emma nodded and stood up. She walked her mom to the door. "Do you have a ride?"

"I called a taxi."

"Mom, that's an expensive trip! I'm sure I can ask Kyle to take you!"

"It's fine, honey. He left for work already and the cab should already be here. I'll call you when I land, and call if you need me."

"I love you, Mom."

"I love you too, honey." Grace grabbed her suitcase and wiped a tear from her cheek before she started off. Emma watched her walk down the hallway before she shut the door and locked it. She was going to lie back on the couch, but instead made her way back to her bedroom. She was going to hang out there for the day.

***

Emma ended up spending the next few days sulking around the apartment. She had contemplated going back to work early but decided that she was going to enjoy the rest of the time off. Micah and her mom leaving in one day, it really took a toll on her.

"Hey, I'm about to hit the mall, wanna come?" Karen asked, poking her head into Emma's room.

"You know, that sounds like a great idea." Emma sighed, pushing herself out of bed.

"Wait," Karen said, putting her hands up in the air.

"What?" Emma looked at her, confused.

"When's the last time you showered?" she joked. Emma began to realize that Karen and Kyle were meant for each other.

"Shut up, I showered...yesterday," Emma informed her.

"Emma! It's nearly three in the afternoon and you still haven't showered?"

"Ugh! Fine. Give me thirty minutes?" Emma stomped across the room toward her bathroom.

"Yeah," she chuckled, closing the bedroom door.

Emma wasn't sure what the big deal was. She brushed her teeth, she just hadn't done anything else. As Emma grabbed her outfit from the closet, tossing it on her bed, she heard a soft knock on the door. "C'mon in," she hollered.

Kyle poked his head in. "Hey, I hear you and Karen are going to the mall?"

"Yeah! I'm kinda excited to have a girly day."

"Well, don't be a douche canoe to her, please."

"A *what*?" Emma cackled.

"A douche canoe. It's the word of the day. Anyway, just be nice, okay?"

"I like Karen! She seems like a sweet girl who doesn't have the IQ of a pretzel!" Emma giggled. Kyle shook his head, trying his hardest not to laugh. "I promise that I'll be nice, though."

"Thank you. Your room smells like ass, when's the last time you showered?"

"Jesus, are you and Karen feeding each other lines? I took a shower yesterday and I'm getting in the shower now, so get out!"

"Just sayin'…"

"Go!" Emma shouted.

Kyle chuckled as he left the room and shut the door behind him. Emma quickly hopped into the shower. She really was excited to have a girls' day out. The last time that she had gone out was a couple years ago, and she couldn't even remember what they had done. Come to think of it, Emma couldn't even remember the girls that she went out with. Today, she was more than happy to get out and have a little fun.

Emma finished up getting ready, and hurried into the living room to find Karen giving Kyle a long, sweet kiss. "Oops, sorry," Emma stated, turning her back.

"You all set?" Karen asked, pushing herself away from Kyle's embrace.

"Yeah. I didn't mean to interrupt you two."

"You're fine, I was just saying bye," Karen responded, grabbing her purse.

"You girls have fun. Remember, if you feel the need to kiss or get naked, take pictures," Kyle chimed in.

"God, you're such a pig!" Emma scoffed.

"Gross, babe." Karen gave him a look of disgust as she followed Emma out the door. Emma locked the door and they made their way to Karen's black Scion. "You ready to go spend some money?" Karen asked, unlocking doors.

"Let's do some damage," Emma insisted as she sat down in the passenger seat.

As they walked around the mall, Emma learned a little bit about Karen. She was an only child, but she hung out with all the boys. She definitely knew how to handle herself. Emma made a mental note to never pick a fight with Karen. She also learned that Karen and Kyle met through one of her skank friends. Her friend was trying to get in with Kyle, but he had to help Karen get away from an asshole at the bar. They really hit it off from there.

"Do you want to grab any coffee?" Emma asked, pointing to the Starbucks.

"Nah, I'm good. I'll go with you though, if you want some."

"Yeah, I'm going to grab a tea. You don't mind?"

"No, I'm just glad to hang out with a girl who doesn't try to hit on everything with a dick," Karen said bluntly.

Emma laughed so hard she snorted. "You and Kyle have been spending way too much time together!"

"Why do you say that?"

"'Cause that would be something he would say. Do a lot of your friends troll the mall?"

"They would troll the middle of nowhere if they thought they'd have a chance to find a hot guy."

"Wow. Maybe it's a good thing I don't have a lot of girlfriends."

"I don't really have a lot of girlfriends, to be honest. I have just a few who are going through a phase where they seem to think they should find a guy who wants to spoil them rotten and whisk them away."

"How's that going for them?"

"They're still single and going to the club every night."

Emma cringed as she stepped up to order her tea. "Can I get a black iced tea, grande?" she asked the barista.

"Two dollars and thirty-four cents. Can I get a name?" he asked, pulling out a plastic cup.

"D. Canoe," Emma replied, laughing. He gave her the strangest of looks as he wrote down the 'name' she had given.

"D. Canoe?" Karen asked.

"Kyle called me a douche canoe earlier and I'm totally in love with it."

Karen laughed so hard that she had to wipe tears from her eyes. "That is by far the best thing that I've heard!"

"Right?" Emma grabbed her iced tea from the counter and they made their way back into the mall. It seemed that they had similar tastes in clothing and department stores. Emma was having a blast hanging out with Karen. She began to pray that

Kyle's dumb ass would keep her around.

They walked into a new store that Emma hadn't even heard of that consisted of lingerie on one half of the store and then toys in the back corner of the store. Karen was interested in picking out something sexy for Kyle, and all Emma could think of was the fact that she was going to have to invest in batteries again. Emma didn't know why she couldn't let the idea of 'Micah helped her dad find her and now he wanted to kill her' get through her thick skull. She just continued to think about how much she enjoyed being around Micah.

"I'm going to step outside," Emma whispered to Karen, who was holding up a corset to her chest.

"Are you okay?" Karen carefully placed the corset back on the shelf.

"Oh yeah, just a little warm in here," Emma lied, pushing open the door. With spring quickly approaching, it was nice to enjoy the weather without a heavy coat. However, in Colorado, one nice day didn't mean the snow was gone for good.

Emma took a seat on one of the benches in the courtyard and sipped on her tea. Some kids were playing tag around some of the chairs that were set up on the fake grassy area. She decided to have a little fun and use her powers on the big kid who was being chased by the smaller kid. Emma began to concentrate and made the big kid stop in his tracks and watched him get tagged. She could hear him ask what had just happened and all the kids looked at him like he was crazy. She couldn't help but chuckle to herself.

"Is this seat taken?" a male voice with some sort

of accent asked. Emma looked up and saw a good-looking man standing at the end of the bench. He was looking at his cell phone and hadn't even bothered to really make eye contact.

"Y-yes. I mean no, it's not taken," Emma stuttered.

"Thanks," he replied, sitting down on the edge as he continued to check his phone.

"Great weather we're having, huh?" As soon as the words poured out, she wanted to smack herself. *Great weather?*

"Uh, yeah. It's actually a bit better than where I'm from."

"Where are you from?"

"London." He finally looked up from the screen and made eye contact with Emma. His green eyes sparkled in the sunlight.

"Oh, I've always wanted to go!" Emma said a little too enthusiastically. She wanted to run away right then.

"What's your name?" he asked, scooting toward her.

"Emma."

"Beautiful name," he said, smiling. "I'm Mason."

"Nice to meet you." Emma tried to hide her cheesy smile by drinking her tea.

"Emma, I don't usually do this, but can I get your number?"

"Uh…you never ask a girl for her number? Really? That's the best you got?" Emma scoffed. He looked embarrassed.

"She'd love to," Karen answered from behind

her. Emma shot around on the bench and gave her a glare. Karen pulled out a piece of paper and a pen, handing them to Emma. She jotted her number down, reminding herself to kick Karen's ass when this gorgeous guy was gone—even though Emma knew she'd lose. Emma handed the piece of paper to him and blushed.

"Brilliant. I'm supposed to be meeting a few of my mates right now, so I'll speak to you soon?"

"O-okay," Emma stuttered. She couldn't help but watch him walk away. He began to remove his leather jacket and revealed tattoos down his left arm. "Oh. My. God. What did you just get me into?" Emma slapped Karen's arm as she sat down next to her.

"I got you into that total hottie's arms! Look, I don't know much about the last guy you dated, but Kyle said you guys were pretty hot and heavy. He also said that some crazy shit has gone on, so to see you just locking yourself in that stank bedroom of yours is not healthy. Time to meet new people!"

"I don't know," Emma said hesitantly.

"All you did was give the guy your number."

"Wow, I've only known you for a short time and you're already pimping me out." Emma chuckled.

"Better believe it. Come on, Express is having a sale," she stated, pulling Emma's arm. They walked back inside the mall and up toward the store. "We gotta find you something hot to wear."

***

As Emma zipped the side of the black pencil

skirt, she could hear her phone buzzing inside her jeans pocket. She quickly reached down to see Micah's name pop up on the screen. She sighed as she pushed *ignore*. It was quickly followed by another call from him. She decided to answer this time.

"Micah…" Emma was a little shocked that he was calling. "What's up?"

"Where are you?"

"I'm at the mall. What's the matter?" Emma was worried

"I was going to leave today, but I talked to Ying this morning. I think you should head home."

"What did she have to say? I'm fine! I'm just out shopping."

"Your dad. He's hired someone else, but this time to kill you…"

Emma thought she was going to pass out in the middle of the fitting room. The room became really small and she found it hard to catch her breath. "W-what? W-what do you mean he's sent someone to kill me?"

"Emma, he doesn't want it on his hands. He just wants you gone."

"I need to go…" Emma gasped.

"Emma, I'm coming to…"

Emma quickly interrupted. "No, Micah! I'm going to handle this on my own," she snapped, and hung the phone up. Emma took a seat on the cold bench in the fitting room and tried to process everything.

"Em? You okay?" Karen asked, knocking on the door.

Emma took a deep breath. "Yeah, I'll be out in a second. I'm really digging this skirt."

"I wanna see when you're dressed."

"All right." Emma couldn't let Micah continue to interfere with everything. She stood up and put a coral sweater on before straightening out the skirt. "You ready?" she asked, opening the door.

"Yes! I'm excited to see!" Karen said. Emma was just as excited to show her. And the fact that Emma had a *girl* shopping buddy was exciting. Emma stepped out of the room to see Karen smiling. "Oh, Emma, that looks perfect on you! I have a perfect pair of slingback kitten heels that would look great with it!"

"You don't think it's a little much? I guess I could wear it to work. I just…don't dress up this much."

"Hmm, it looks really nice, but if you don't dress up, you might be right. How about this sweater, a pair of jeans, and the heels?"

"I think that would be more…me." Emma smiled and headed back into the fitting room. The thought of Karen being around to help her was a great feeling. Emma was having so much fun. She heard her phone buzzing along the bench. "Ugh."

"Ex problems?" Karen asked, peeking over her shoulder at the phone.

"Yeah…" Emma sighed, walking toward her phone. This time it wasn't Micah's number, it was an unknown number. Emma quickly answered, "Hello?"

"Hiya, is this Emma?" the male voice asked.

"It is? Who is this?"

"It's Mason, umm we met not too long ago at the mall."

"Oh! Hi!" she exclaimed. His accent was so incredibly sexy.

"So, I was thinking…I'd love to take you to grab a bite to eat or some coffee."

"Really?" Emma asked, surprised.

"I would. I met up with my mates and they were chatting up a few ladies and I couldn't seem to stop thinking about you."

"Wow, layin' down the pick-up lines already?" she joked. Karen walked up toward Emma to put her ear close to the phone.

"It sounds rubbish, I know, but I really wished I could've continued talking to you."

"Well, I'm free next…" Emma started, but Karen quickly pinched her arm. "Ow!"

"You all right?" he asked.

"Yeah, sorry, I…I'm free tonight."

"Wonderful! So I'll make things a little less formal, seeing as how you just met me in the courtyard, and I'll meet you at the Yard House. Say seven?"

"Sure, that'll be great. I'll see you then."

"Goodbye, Emma," he purred.

"Bye, Mason." Emma hung up and turned toward Karen. "I have a date tonight!" she screeched.

"A hot one at that!" Karen clapped. "I think that this sweater would be amazing for the date! Let's get you a new pair of jeans and maybe a new bra."

"A new bra? Why would I need a new bra?"

"Hello? Second base?" Karen laughed, grabbing

her own chest.

"You and Kyle were seriously meant for each other!" Emma chuckled, smacking Karen's arm. Emma walked back into the fitting room and shut the door behind her. She began to plot her outfit along with the new bra she was about to purchase.

They walked down toward Victoria's Secret at the other end of the mall, laughing and joking about funny moments with Kyle. Although Emma had 'vaulted' the moment in college when Kyle got shoved out of the dorm showers, butt naked, by a dude and his girlfriend looking for a place to have sex and had to run to the other side of the building to Emma's room—it was too good not to share. Emma thought she was going to pee her pants after that story. He was going to kill her.

Karen then shared the story about how on the night they had met, her dog thought it would be fun to join in on the action. Mugs, her five pound Chihuahua, decided to lick Kyle's left ass cheek. Tears were streaming down Emma's face from laughing so hard. Needless to say, Kyle didn't like to go over to Karen's place as much.

"Kyle wouldn't think it was as funny, being the reason we're laughing so hard," Emma breathed out. Her stomach was hurting so hard. She tried to browse through the selections of push up bras as she caught her breath.

"No, but I'm glad that we are laughing at his expense." Karen sighed, wiping a tear from her eye.

"Me too. Karen, thank you so much for taking me with you. After my mom headed back, I really needed a cheer up."

"I don't think it was just your mom leaving. Can I ask what happened with you and the last guy?"

"Micah." Emma sighed. "He lied to me and I really thought that we had clicked…"

"You can't forgive him?"

"I really wanted to. I still do. I don't know what to do! I feel like if I forgive him, he's going to walk all over me like every other guy I've ever been with."

"That's true, but you don't know. He might be different."

Emma sighed and rubbed her temples. This whole situation with Micah was one that she'd never understand. "He might be. I just need to figure out some other shit before I ever consider the thought."

"Other things? Emma, I hate to be nosy, but after you were out for two days…I'm kinda dying to know what happened."

"You wouldn't believe me if I told you." Emma really liked Karen, but she didn't know how she was even going to explain that she's a witch.

"Try me!" Karen placed the bra back on the rack. The only way Emma was going to be able to really explain was to show her. Emma took a deep breath in and reached for a pair of underwear on the table across from them. As the undergarment began to lift off the table and move toward them, Karen's smile began to fade. "What. The. Hell?"

"Told you." Emma nervously chuckled.

"That's amazing! How'd you do that?" Karen asked, smacking Emma's arm.

"How about if I tell you on the way home if you

help me find a really pretty bra?"

"Deal!" Karen exclaimed, rushing around, grabbing several bras around them. "How about one of these?"

Emma chuckled, searching through the pile in Karen's arms. "I like this one. Does it have matching underwear?"

Chapter Six

After Karen and Emma had finished up their shopping, Emma kept her promise and explained to Karen what had happened in the store. She didn't say much to Emma the whole ride home, but she did listen and thankfully didn't look at Emma like she was completely insane. As they pulled up to Emma's building, Karen didn't park or turn off the engine.

"Are you not coming up?" Emma asked, unbuckling the seatbelt.

"No, I…" Karen started.

"Shit, Karen, I didn't scare you off, did I? Please don't hold this against Kyle!" Emma panicked. She really felt bad that she unloaded too much on Karen.

"Emma, it's fine! I have work really early in the morning and parent-teacher conferences all day, so I had already planned on heading home after."

"Are you sure you're not completely freaked out?" Emma asked.

"Oh it's a little weird, but no, I'm not completely freaked out." She chuckled.

"Okay. Well, thanks again for taking me with you."

"It was a lot of fun! We should totally do it again!"

"I'd really like that." Emma smiled, opened her door, and stepped out. As she shut the door behind her, she waved goodbye before running up the outside stairs and into the building. Emma couldn't wait to commend Kyle for picking Karen. She dashed up the stairs and quickly unlocked the door, but as she tried to open it, she realized something was blocking it.

"Hey, wait!" Kyle shouted. Emma peeked in the cracked open door to find a ladder and Kyle in front of the door.

"What are you doing?" she asked, sliding through the opening.

"The damn smoke detector was chirping and making me slowly lose my mind, so…oh shit!" His footing started to slip and Kyle began to fall. Without even trying, Emma used her powers to break his fall, slowly lowering him to the ground. "Jesus! Thanks, Emma."

"Are you okay?" She breathed hard, squatting down next to him.

"Yeah. Fucking vaulted ceilings. Thanks for…holy shit, you used your magic on me!"

"You're just now realizing this? You think that I could catch you?"

Kyle pushed himself off the floor. "Well, I guess it's better than that mean shit that you pulled on me when you first used your magic."

"Are you really going to hold that against me for

the rest of my life?” Emma scoffed.

“Probably.” He smiled and nudged her arm. “Hey, how’d things go with Karen?”

“She really is awesome. I’m glad you are with her. But…” Emma paused, taking a few steps away from Kyle as she prepared for the worst.

“What’d you do?” he asked with a sigh.

“Nothing! I…I showed her my magic,” Emma said quietly.

“Why’d you do that?” he panicked.

“I’m not really ashamed of it. I thought that I had to hide it, but now I’m fine with people knowing. Don’t get me wrong, I’m not going on Maury anytime soon and bragging about it.”

“I think Maury will only let you on if you need to find yo’ babies’ daddy,” Kyle joked.

Emma noticed the time on the clock and smacked her forehead. “Damn it! Oh! Shit, I need to get ready!”

“Ready? For what?” Kyle curiously asked.

“Nosy!” she exclaimed, walking toward her room. Kyle began to follow her and stopped at the door before she could close it on him. “Hey, I’m trying to change!” she shouted.

“You’re not going out with Micah, are you?” Kyle scolded.

“No. He…I’m done with him. I actually got asked out by this guy at the mall.” Emma was beaming at the thought of Mason.

“Oh yeah? Scamming for guys at the mall?”

“Shut up! Oh, and get this, he’s English!” She smiled widely, trying her hardest at an English accent.

"So where is Austin Powers taking you?" Kyle joked.

"Oh my God, I'm done talking to you!" Emma scoffed, pushing him out of the doorway and slamming the door.

"Aww, c'mon! I was just messin'!" he hollered from behind the closed door. Emma ignored him and set her bags down on the bed before undressing. Thanks to Kyle, she wasn't going to be able to get the image of Austin Powers out of her head and prayed that she didn't start spouting off movie lines during dinner. "Groovy, baby!" she exclaimed, snipping the tags off of her new sweater and jeans, looking over her outfit. "Shit!" Emma shook her head, realizing she was reciting movie lines now. She was screwed.

*****

"Welcome to the Yard House. Are you meeting anyone?" the very flamboyant host asked, holding the door open for Emma as she walked in.

"Uh, yeah. I'm a few minutes early…"

"Emma!" Mason greeted, shouting over the loud crowd from the bar. He was surrounded by a bunch of people who she only assumed were friends. This wasn't a date after all. Her stomach twisted into knots.

"That's my…the guy I'm meeting," she said, smiling at the host. He gave her a nod as she walked toward Mason. "Hi. Are those all your…mates?" Emma asked. She suddenly wanted to crawl into a hole. She should've just said friends.

"Them? No, some really great people I met just waiting at the bar. They're betting on your baseball team. They have had *way* too much to drink and offered to buy me a beer. You Americans are rather friendly after a few pints." He chuckled. God, he was gorgeous. "You ready to eat?"

Emma nodded as he placed his hand on her lower back, guiding her to the table he had near the bar. He even smelled good. He had brownie points across the board—smelled nice, gentleman, and, best of all, she didn't get any sense of magic or bad feelings from him.

Even though it was kind of loud from the people at the bar and the baseball game they had broadcasting, she felt like when he was talking to her, she was the only one in the restaurant with him. His accent alone was melting her panties. "So, uh, Mason. What brings you to America?"

"Football. I played for a team back home and I was brought out here to try out for a few teams."

Emma looked at him, surprised; he was muscular, but she couldn't picture him playing football. "You have a tryout with the Broncos, then?"

"Pardon? Oh, sorry, you lot call it soccer." He chuckled.

"Oh! Sorry. Well, that's great. How are those going?" Emma made a mental note to look up all of the English words and their meanings when she got home. She felt like an idiot.

"Really well, actually. I've been to Chicago, Portland, and DC. So far, this is by far the best offer. Enough about me, what about you? Are you from Colorado?"

"No, I'm an import as well. I grew up in Massachusetts and came out here for college. I met my roommate and we decided to stay out here. I love it, it's beautiful."

Mason stared deeply into Emma's eyes. "It really is beautiful. Maybe it's just because of you."

Emma blushed. "Wow, you've got some great pick-up lines."

"I don't use pick-up lines, Emma," Mason said. "I just say what's going to make you smile."

She melted into the bench and watched him smile at her. Before she could say anything further, their waiter came over to take their order. Mason ordered them an appetizer of artichoke dip and decided to have a burger. Emma agreed the burger sounded good. They both also ended up ordering the same beer. Emma liked the way they agreed on the food.

"So, Mason, what have you done that is fun out here?" Emma asked, playing with her napkin.

"You have beautiful hiking areas, but by far meeting this girl and her agreeing to a dinner with me was the best." He paused as their waiter set down the beers and artichoke dip. "Cheers, mate," Mason said to the waiter. Emma couldn't help but smile widely at this gorgeous man. "So, what were we saying?" he asked Emma.

"Uh…"

"That's right, I was going to ask if I could see you again."

"Mason, we haven't even finished dinner." Emma chuckled.

"I'm trying to get it out of the way so that way it's not completely awkward to ask you later."

"I think we can meet up again," Emma said.

Chapter Seven

The rest of the evening, Emma enjoyed her time with Mason and for once didn't feel like she had to impress him with her powers or talk only about magic. With Mason, she really felt relaxed. They stayed at the restaurant until closing time, learning about one another.

"Mason, I really had a great time," Emma said as they walked toward the parking lot.

"I as well. I really can't wait to see you again," Mason stated as he slowly reached for Emma's hand.

"Well, I'm off work tomorrow and the rest of the weekend…" Emma started.

"Perfect! I'll pick you up tomorrow. What are your thoughts on hiking?"

Emma had yet to go up to any sort of trails or mountains since moving to Colorado, so she wasn't fully opposed to the thought, but she had been so inactive that she was going to look totally out of shape. "My thoughts? I think that I'd die." She giggled.

"Nah, I wouldn't let that happen. How's about I give you a ring in the morning and we can plan a day of it?"

How could Emma say no to someone so gorgeous and talking to her with a British accent? "All right," she said before he leaned in and placed a soft kiss on her lips. Her whole body flushed as his soft lips caressed hers.

"Good night, Emma. I'll speak to you in the morning," he whispered as he pulled away from her. Emma couldn't even muster up the words to say anything back. She stood in the parking lot of the restaurant, feeling amazing.

The entire drive home she felt as if she were on a whole other planet. Emma quickly parked Kyle's SUV in his spot and hurried upstairs. She couldn't wait to tell him about her date.

"Ky?" she shouted, opening the front door.

"My room," he hollered back. Emma skipped down the hallway to Kyle's room. He was lying on his bed, writing in his work notebook. "How was the date with Austin Powers? Did he make you horny, baby?" He chuckled.

Emma glared at him. "You're such an ass. But the date went great, he's…he's really great." Emma sighed.

"So you finally gonna stop sulking over Micah?" Kyle asked, sitting up.

"I don't know, I guess."

"It'll be for the best, Em. So you like this new guy?"

"Yeah, he seems really nice and someone I could get to know!"

"Em, serious question…" Kyle started.

"Oh great, what?"

"Since you know all these powers and this guy you say is from England…do you think you guys will have a chance to get the kid into Hogwarts?" Kyle burst with laughter.

"You're so dumb!" Emma joked, slapping Kyle's leg before she walked out of his room.

"Oh come on! Valid question!" Kyle hollered at her.

Emma walked down the hall to her room. She sat down on her bed and began to wonder how she would tell Mason about her powers. Would she even tell him? He was going to find out soon enough, though. She remembered Micah telling her that you didn't tell everyone *everything*. Emma sighed as she kicked off her shoes. Switching on her TV, she got comfortable and flipped through a few channels before her phone began to ring.

"Hello?" she answered.

"Emma?" the male voice responded. She knew right then it was Mason. "It's Mason. I'm so sorry to call you at a late hour, but I wanted to make sure you arrived home safely."

Emma smiled widely, trying her hardest not to act too giddy. "That's very sweet of you, Mason. I did. Thank you again for tonight, I really did have a great time."

"I did too. So, I was thinking, since you weren't so keen on the idea of hiking, how about breakfast?"

"I think I'd like that a lot more." Emma giggled.

"I'll be around about ten?"

"That's perfect. I'll see you in the morning, Mason."

"Good night, Emma," he purred. Emma hung up the phone and squealed. The way he said her name made her melt. She was going to have the hardest time falling asleep now—she was way too excited. She peeked out of her room to see if Kyle was still awake. She needed to find out when Karen was going to come by next—she really had to thank her for giving her number to Mason—but his light was out in his room.

Emma sighed, heading back into her room. She'd just have to wait until morning. Turning the TV off, she picked up one of her magic books. As much as she wanted to continue her happiness with a new guy and trying to go on with being 'normal,' the fact remained that her dad was still out there and he still wanted to hurt her. She read about safety spells until her eyes became heavy.

***

"You really don't think you can save everyone, do you?" Sebastian chuckled.

"I will. I can't let you hurt anyone!" Emma breathed heavily, trying to stand up. She felt weak, she couldn't feel her powers at her fingertips anymore. "Please…"

"Just give me what I want and nobody else has to die!" he demanded.

"No!" she screamed.

***

"Emma! Wake up!" Kyle shouted, shaking her.

"Kyle! He's going to kill someone! I can't let him!" Emma awoke in a sweat. "Oh my God, Kyle, what if he tries to hurt you?"

"Emma, he's not going to hurt anyone. I won't let him." Kyle wiped the tears from Emma's cheeks. "So, uh, did you have a breakfast date with Aus—I mean Mason?"

"Yeah, why?" Emma asked, puzzled. "Why aren't you at work?"

"'Cause he's here. And I took the day off. I've been working some crazy hours lately and I needed a day away from the office."

Emma jumped out of bed in a panic. "What! Oh fuck! Please tell him I'll be out in a few!" Emma shouted, running into her bathroom. She quickly showered, and with the help of her magic she was able to do her hair and makeup in one sitting. Today she was more thankful than ever to have the ability to do such things, but as she used her powers she realized this was something she wasn't going to keep hidden. Emma finished getting ready, the fastest she had ever done in probably her entire life, and ran out of her room to greet Mason.

Mason was sitting on the sofa, talking to Kyle about sports when Emma came down the hall. She was happy to see Kyle hitting it off with him. She soon found herself thinking of Micah and what he was doing. As soon as that thought crossed her mind, she shook her head and tried to rid any thoughts of him.

"Mason, I am *so* sorry!" Emma stated.

"No worries, love. You ready?" he asked, standing from the sofa.

Emma smiled and nodded. "Hey, Ky, will you give Karen my number? I need her to call me later."

"Sure. I should be seeing her later. You kids have fun today. Don't do anything I wouldn't do." He chuckled.

"Shut up," Emma scolded. Mason gave Emma a puzzled look. "He's special," Emma joked.

Mason grabbed ahold of Emma's hand as they walked out of her apartment and toward his car. Everything about him was so different and she enjoyed that, but now she was going to have to tell him about her powers and change everything.

"So, my mates have been on about this crepe place not too far from here. You ever been?" Mason asked, opening the car door.

"I haven't. You know, I kinda stick to the familiar stuff. Pizza, beer, fast food." Emma laughed nervously. "That sounded like I'm addicted to junk food and an alcoholic, huh?"

Mason laughed. "No, back home there were only a couple takeaway places I'd stick to. Here I figure, 'when in Rome,' or in this case, Denver."

"Very logical. Well, let's go."

Mason shut her door and slid into the driver's seat. Sitting next to him made her feel a little giddy inside.

They parked along the outside of the restaurant and Mason made sure that Emma didn't open her door. She was truly impressed by his chivalry as he kept ahold of her hand as they walked into the café.

"Morning!" the waitress greeted as they took a seat at their table.

"Hi," Emma responded, smiling.

"I'm Imogen. What can I get for you?"

"I'll take a coffee," Emma said.

"Make it two," Mason agreed. He set the menu down and looked to Emma. "I know this is weird, but I hope it doesn't sound rushed."

"Oh, no. What?" Emma asked hesitantly.

"I really feel relaxed with you," Mason said, smiling.

Emma smiled widely. She knew the moment she told him about her being a witch was going to change that, but for now she felt the same. "Mason, that's very sweet. I feel the same. I feel like I can talk to you about anything."

The waitress returned with two mugs of coffee. "You ready to order?" Imogen asked.

"I might need an extra second," Emma said, looking up from the menu. Imogen nodded and walked away. "I'm sorry. Everything looks so good."

"I agree. I can't decide if I want breakfast or these crepes with ice cream!"

"No way, I was thinking the same thing." Emma chuckled. "I think I might go with the ice cream. It is milk, right? Oh great, they have some with Bailey's. There's me going on about alcohol again." Emma laughed.

"I was just eyeing that one as well. Make you a deal, I'll order the one with alcohol so you don't feel as bad, and you get the plain ice cream one and we'll share. Deal?"

Emma nodded. Imogen made her way back and they ordered their meals. Emma watched up at the bar as the crepes were being handmade. She really enjoyed how sweet Mason was to her, but it didn't stop her from thinking about Micah. It was true, Micah was going to be the only guy who really understood her powers and her being a witch. And now, Emma wasn't sure she wanted to share her powers with Mason. She knew it wasn't going to be something that people handled lightly, and she didn't want to scare him away already.

"Everything okay over there?" Mason asked, grabbing Emma's hand.

"Yeah," Emma replied with a smile, snapping out of her daze.

"You looked like you had a bit on your mind. Hope I'm not boring you already," Mason joked.

"Oh, no, not at all. So, have you thought anymore about what team you might sign with?" Emma asked as their crepes were placed in front of them.

"I'm liking Colorado the most," he said, smiling.

Emma blushed. Not only was his accent dreamy, his smiling at her really made her giddy. "How's it taste?" she asked, watching Mason take a bite.

"My mates didn't steer me wrong with this place. It's really good. How's yours?"

Emma took a bite of her crepe and all of her taste buds had a party. "This is amazing!" As she savored the food, Mason scooted his chair next to her and slid his plate next to her.

"Here, try this one," he suggested, holding his fork in front of her mouth. She slowly leaned forward and took a bite off his fork. Her eyes didn't leave his. "You really are beautiful, Emma." Mason leaned in and gave Emma a soft kiss on her lips. "And delicious as well."

Emma blushed and giggled as she reached across the table for the cream. It wasn't until it slid across the table to her that she realized she had used her magic. Her eyes darted to Mason, who was looking down at the time. She sighed with relief that she didn't have to explain her powers right away and made a mental note to be careful with what she was doing around him.

As they continued to eat, Emma was excited with this new experience, but at the same time wanted to make sure to take things a little slow with Mason. "Hey, Mason…" Emma started, clearing her throat. "I'm really having a great time with you, but I…I just got out of a relationship and…"

"As did I," he interrupted.

"Oh, well…I just want to make sure that I don't rush into things and make this a total rebound."

Mason sighed. "I completely understand. I really do enjoy your company and would like to see how things go. Slow?"

"That'd be really nice," Emma agreed.

"Right. So, with us taking it slow—I don't want to mess this up, but I have to kiss you again. Would that be all right?"

Emma laughed. "Yeah, that would be more than okay."

Mason leaned in again, cupped Emma's face, and kissed her. The kiss started off really soft and Emma thought that he was going to stop there, but it became more intense. She reached up and combed her hands through his hair. So much for taking things slow—she wanted him more than ever.

72

Chapter Eight

After they had finished enjoying their crepes and several kisses, Emma and Mason took a walk around downtown. Mason held her hand the entire time. Now that she knew about Mason just getting out of a relationship too, she wasn't as nervous that things were going to be rushed. She did want to know what happened, but would wait to ask that question. As they walked, Emma's phone buzzed in her pocket.

Kyle: Hey, beer and pizza night. Karen will be there—wanna bring your dude?

Kyle had perfect timing. "Mason, how'd you like to come over to my place for a beer and pizza? It'll be my roommate and his girlfriend. He just asked if you wanted to join."

"I'd like to, but…"

"No, that's cool," Emma interrupted.

"Oh, I wasn't turning it down. I just was going to say I have practice tomorrow morning, so I would have to leave kind of early. Would that still be okay?"

Emma chuckled. She felt dumb for assuming right away. "Yes, of course!"

"Would you like to come to practice?" he asked nervously.

"Uh. I don't want to get in the way."

"Oh you won't. I'd love to see you there."

"Then I'd love to go. So, you don't mind coming over tonight?" Emma asked, pulling up her messages.

"No, not at all." Mason smiled. Emma quickly sent Kyle a message saying Mason would be there and to be on his best behavior. She also couldn't wait to thank Karen in person for giving Mason her number. She would've chickened out or thought too much about Micah to do it.

"Let's head that way and we can claim our spot on the couch," Emma joked. She and Mason headed back toward his car and drove to her apartment. As Mason drove down the road and waited for the light rail train to pass, Emma thought she saw Micah on the other side of the train, talking to a guy who resembled her father. Her heart stopped and she gasped. Once the train passed she didn't see anyone standing there.

"You okay?" Mason asked, rubbing her shoulder.

"Yeah, I'm sorry. I thought I saw someone I knew. It wasn't them, though."

"No worries. Sorry, but is it this turn?" Mason asked, slowing at a corner.

"Oh, next one. On the left," Emma directed,

hoping she could shake the feeling that maybe Micah wasn't done working for her dad.

Mason pulled into a parking spot and they slowly made their way up to her apartment. Emma could tell he was a little nervous, but she grabbed his hand and gently squeezed and gave him a smile.

When they reached upstairs, Kyle was on the phone. He waved to the two of them before he rushed to his room and shut the door. Emma could hear him yelling at someone, but couldn't hear exactly what he was saying.

"Can I get you a beer?" Emma asked, opening the fridge.

"I'd love one, cheers," Mason answered, walking into the kitchen. Emma opened the bottle and handed it to him.

"Sorry, guys, you'd think after several months of not hearing from me some chicks would get the point," Kyle stated, walking into the kitchen. He took Emma's beer from her hands and took a quick chug.

"Well, here, have a beer!" Emma said, scowling.

"Sorry. I needed that. Fucking Zoe called me!"

"She what?" Emma choked as she took a sip of the beer. Mason watched from the side, confused. "Sorry, Mason. Zoe is a crazy chick that dated Kyle for about a minute and…well, she's just crazy."

"This is how crazy she is: she called to tell me that she saw a pic of me and Karen on Facebook and didn't know that I'd moved on so quickly!" Kyle saw Mason look puzzled. "Dude, I'm not on Facebook! Karen has an account!"

"Damn, mate. I'd steer clear of that one!"

"I'm definitely trying. Anyway, didn't mean to start the night off like that. Karen should be here in a few. She's bringing some more beer and it's your turn to buy pizza, Em."

Emma scoffed. "Hey, last weekend I didn't get any of that pizza, so technically it's still your turn!"

"Nope, still your turn," Kyle stated as he grabbed a beer out of the fridge.

"Fine. Mason, do you like or not like anything specific on your pizza? We tend to just get everything," Emma said as she grabbed her phone out of her pocket. She noticed that she had a message.

"Oh I'm not picky. Please, get what you guys usually get."

"All right, well, go make yourself comfortable while I order the pizza," Emma stated, smiling at Mason. He leaned in and kissed her cheek before heading into the living room. Emma quickly pulled up her messages, hoping that it was from Micah, but instead saw it was from her mom.

Hey, sweetie, just wanted to make sure you were okay. I haven't heard from you in a while. I'm finally getting up to date with texting. I love you lots!

She quickly replied.

Hi, Mom! I'm fine. Just been hanging out. I'll give you a call in the morning. I love you too!

After she pressed *send*, she dialed up the pizza

place and ordered the usual. She was glad that she had a place that recognized her phone number and knew everything she and Kyle wanted. As she hung up, she could hear Kyle and Mason chatting in the other room. Emma almost felt like she had been neglecting her powers, and the urge to use them was pressing at her fingertips. She figured since everyone was in the other room, she'd get the plates and beer using her powers.

"Can I get you another beer, mate?" Mason asked, coming nearer. Emma panicked and quickly grabbed the plates from levitating in front of her. She nearly dropped the four plates as Mason rounded the corner. "Oh, hey, you all right?" he asked, helping her grab the plates.

"Yeah, I just about tripped over my own foot!" Emma lied.

"Well, let me help you. Can I get anything else?" Mason asked, taking the plates to the table.

"No, I think I'm finally good. Pizza should be here in a few minutes. You and Kyle doing okay in there?" Emma asked as she took another beer from the fridge.

"He's really funny. I think he might be a bit obsessed with calling me Austin. I hate to ask, but is that an ex-boyfriend?"

"Oh fuck! Kyle!" Emma shouted. "I'm so sorry. He thinks he's being funny."

"What's up, buttercup?" Kyle happily asked, walking into the kitchen.

"Will you, for fuck's sake, stop calling Mason '*Austin*'? It's not funny!" Emma snapped.

"Oh shit, man, did I actually call you that?" Kyle

asked, embarrassed.

"Twice, but I figured that it was another guy around." Mason took a sip from his beer.

"No, I was joking with Emma…look, man, I'm sorry. I'm an ass." Kyle blushed.

Kyle turned and walked out of the room, but before he rounded the corner he mouthed to Emma that he was sorry. Emma glared at him, but nodded. Mason walked closer to Emma.

"Mason…" she began.

"Shh. It's okay. Can I admit something?" Mason asked, pulling Emma closer to him.

"Umm, sure," she said, looking at him, puzzled.

"You were incredibly sexy, being all shouty with him." Mason chuckled.

Emma blushed at being chest to chest with this incredibly sexy man, who was telling *her* she was sexy. "Wow. Thanks," Emma breathed. Mason then slowly placed a soft kiss on her lips. Rather than taking it slow, Emma wanted nothing more than to rip his clothes off and take advantage of him. The kiss became harder and faster. Mason teased Emma's tongue before he lightly bit her bottom lip.

Mason pushed her up against one of the counters, their hands racing up and down each other's bodies. Emma's powers were once again at her fingertips, and she wanted so badly to push him up against the wall and show him all she could do in the bedroom with her powers.

"Uh-um," Kyle cleared his throat. Emma and Mason quickly straightened themselves up. Emma noticed that Karen was standing next to him, smiling widely.

"Sorry. I didn't hear you guys come in," Emma said, blushing.

"Hi. Mason, right? I'm Karen. We really didn't get a proper introduction yesterday," she said, reaching for his hand.

"Hiya, Karen. I'm sorry, I should've said more to you that day. You were lovely enough to get Emma, here, to give me her number."

"Well, I'm glad things are going well." Karen winked. "I brought beer." Karen opened the fridge and placed two boxes of beer on the shelf. She gave Emma a glance and Emma kind of felt a little weird about the look. She hoped that Karen wasn't feeling any sort of awkwardness about her showing her powers to her.

"Hey, Karen, can I talk to you for a second?" Emma asked quietly. Kyle and Mason each grabbed a beer and walked into the living room.

"What's up?" Karen asked.

"I just want to make sure that you're not...I don't know, uh, weirded out by me."

"Why would you think that?"

"I don't know. I just had this awkward feeling and I hope that it isn't mutual. I'm always trying to hide my powers and then here I am sharing them with you in the middle of the mall!" Emma blurted.

"Oh, sweetie, you're fine! It did take me by surprise, but its fine. I promise." Karen smiled as she patted Emma on the arm. The two of them headed into the living room where the guys were sitting on the couch, watching a soccer game on TV. Emma rolled her eyes as she knew a movie might be out of the question now. Two sports nuts finding a game on TV, with beer. A girlfriend's worst nightmare. Karen sat down and huffed next to Emma. The girls giggled as the guys were completely oblivious to them entering the living room. Emma felt like a normal person now, hanging out with a possible boyfriend, her best friend, and his girlfriend.

***

After the pizza arrived, Kyle finally put on a movie—*The Expendables*, not something that Emma and Karen were too thrilled about. Emma was just happy to have Mason, who wanted to cuddle up on the love seat with her. Once the movie came to an end, Kyle and Karen said their good nights and disappeared into his room. Emma looked at the clock on the mantle and realized it was nearing eleven. She knew her evening with Mason was coming to an end.

"I'm really glad that you came over," Emma stated, yawning.

"Me too, but I should probably head out. I've got to be at the field at nine."

Emma nodded, snuggling into him. Mason lifted her chin and kissed her. She pulled herself up onto him and straddled his legs. They may have been on a smaller love seat, but she was willing to take full advantage of it. "Stay," she whispered as she started to kiss his earlobe.

Mason growled as he pushed into her. Emma rocked her hips on him as he pulled her face to his and kissed her harder and more passionately than she had been kissed in a long time. Mason grabbed Emma and picked her up. "Which way to your room?" he whispered. She pointed to the end of the hall and he carried her in that direction.

With each kiss and each touch of Mason she became more excited, but the lingering feeling of Micah was still present. She started to recall their first moment in her room and the light bursting. Her heart slowly began to ache and yet she was with another incredible guy. One who had the potential to help her realize a normal life was not as bad as she thought.

Mason lay Emma on the bed and removed his shirt. His muscular body and tattoos were incredible to look at. Emma slipped her top off and tossed it across the room. Mason crawled atop Emma and began to kiss from her neck down to her navel. Emma let out a soft moan. This would be the first time for non-magical sex and Emma felt a little nervous, but Mason was making her forget everything.

Emma lifted her hips as Mason slid her pants down. "Mason…"

"I've got protection in my pocket," he stated.

Emma wanted to tell him everything at that moment, but stopped as he removed his pants and boxers. She didn't want to ruin anything with Mason by bringing up magic or anything about Micah. And she did feel a little insulted that he had protection in his pocket. "You brought a condom with you?" she asked.

"Yeah, I always…" Mason stopped as Emma sat up and pushed herself up to the top of the bed.

"Emma, wait, that's not what I meant. I just carried it with me…shit, this is not sounding good for me."

"You're right, it doesn't sound good at all!"

"Can I explain without you getting more upset?" he begged, scooting closer to her. Emma glared at him, not really sure she wanted to hear. She sighed and slowly nodded her head. "So, I'm staying with a few of my mates. I told them what a great time I had with you and when I left this morning they thought it would be funny to line up and each hand me a condom. They wouldn't let me out the door without at least taking one." Mason grabbed Emma's hand as he explained. "I didn't think for one moment that we'd be in this position. I promise."

Emma chuckled as she shook her head. Mason had no reason to lie to her, so she pulled him closer to her and kissed his lips. They both lay on the pillow and he rolled back on top of her, slowly entering her. She moaned as she felt him slide into her. She knew at that moment she was going to have to control any sort of powers she was going to feel. Mason felt incredible as he pushed into her.

Her fingers dug deep into his back as a way to get her mind off of using any sort of magic. He reached up and grabbed her arms, raised them above her head, and held her hands down. "You're so beautiful," he whispered as he lifted his head up and looked down at her.

Emma blushed and smiled as she lifted her head and kissed his lips. As he pushed harder and faster into her, she could feel her orgasm nearing and her powers becoming stronger. She wasn't going to deny the sex was amazing, but it became more intense as she tried to hide her powers.

"Oh God!" she screamed. Her powers finally knocked a frame off her dresser as her hands swished in that direction. Emma gasped as Mason looked over.

"Did you hear something?" he asked.

"No," Emma lied, breathing heavily. "What was it?"

"It sounded like something fell over on your dresser."

Emma shook her head as she looked over at the dresser, pretending to look for something that fell. "Sorry, I didn't hear anything." Emma kissed Mason's shoulder. He looked back at her and smiled.

"Emma, you are truly incredible," Mason stated, rolling off of her and propping himself on his arm next to her. "I really like being with you. Is it weird that I feel this way after a couple of days?"

Emma smiled. "No, I think it's how I feel too." She really was having a great time with him. Even with Micah lingering in the back of her mind, Mason was really great to be around.

"I hate to leave…" he started.

"I know, but I will let you go, just this once," she joked. Mason chuckled as he kissed her once more.

"See you in the morning?" he asked as he dressed.

"Bright and early. Which field?"

"We'll be at…shite, that stadium off Interstate 70? Dick's."

Emma laughed. She really did enjoy hearing

Mason talk. "Okay, I'll be there."

Mason quickly dressed and returned to Emma. He kissed her several times before he snuck out of her room. She waited to hear the door shut behind him and used her magic to lock the door. She giggled as she cuddled into her blankets.

Chapter Nine

Emma was too excited to sleep the entire night. The thought of Mason and their extraordinary night ran through her mind. For once in the last few months, things began to feel normal again. The dreams weren't as constant, and even though her powers were still there, she was not having that dark feeling nearly as much anymore.

She woke up a half hour before the alarm that she had set before bed—she felt like she'd gotten a total of two hours of sleep. She quickly rushed to the bathroom to take a shower and get down to the field. As she stepped out of the shower, Emma could hear her phone faintly ringing. She wrapped the towel around her and ran into her bedroom, but by the time she reached her phone it had already gone to voice mail. She picked up her phone and it came up as an unknown number. She had a feeling in the pit of her stomach that it had been too quiet lately and that the call was going to be something bad. The voice mail icon appeared on her menu. Emma hesitantly pushed it and held her phone up to her ear.

"Hey, Emma, it's Mason. I couldn't sleep at all last night. I only could think about you! Anyway, I'm off to the training headquarters. I hope you'll still be able to make it. Later, love."

Emma giggled as she set her phone down on the bed and started to get dressed. She had no idea what to wear to soccer training, but she still wanted to look cute. She grabbed a pair of jean capris and one of her cute tees. While dressing, she heard a knock at the door.

"Em?" Karen asked behind the door.

"It's open, come on in," Emma hollered, making her way into the bathroom.

"I just wanted to say thanks." Karen took a seat on the edge of the bed as Emma poked her head around the corner.

"For what?"

"I had a great time hanging out with you guys last night and I…I really like hanging out with all of us."

"Oh, Karen, I do too. What brought this up?"

"I just didn't have a lot of friends when I was younger and as I get older I realize which friends are really there for me. Just being emotional, I guess."

"Well, I'm glad you're around. I enjoy hanging out with you and having you as a friend. You make Kyle really happy and you helped me in the biggest way possible." Emma paused as Karen gave her a puzzled look. "I had been really down about my mom *and* Micah leaving. You took me out and gave a really great guy my number."

"You two do look like you're hitting it off," Karen added, smiling.

"We are. I'm actually heading out to watch his soccer training. Last night was just amazing."

"Well, I'm really happy for you. Thanks for listening to me get all emotional." Karen chuckled, standing up.

"Of course. Let's hang out again soon." Emma waved to Karen as she headed out of her room and ran into the bathroom to finish getting ready. She had already been late once meeting up with Mason, she didn't want it to be a trend.

After Emma was fully satisfied with the way she looked, she grabbed her phone and her purse off her bed and dashed for the front door. Kyle was standing in the kitchen, drinking some coffee.

"Hey, where you in a hurry to?" he asked, poking his head out of the kitchen.

"I'm going to watch Mason practice," Emma rushed to say.

"I guess you're taking my car?" Kyle asked snidely.

"Oh, yeah. I'm sorry. Look, Monday after work, will you take me down to a dealership and help me get something?"

"Hell yeah. I'm glad I didn't have any plans, dick," Kyle joked. "Call me when you get on the road. I know you're in a rush, but I need to ask you something."

"All right. Talk in a few." Emma rushed out the door and hurried to Kyle's SUV. She started down the road and once she got on the highway she pulled her phone out of her bag and dialed Kyle. "What's up?" she asked as he answered.

"Was Karen acting really weird to you this morning?" he asked.

"Yeah, kinda, but I'm a chick, so I get it. Why?"

"Dude, I think she has become obsessed with the fact that you have powers. All she kept asking me this morning was about how you use them and if I think you use them all the time. I don't know, it kinda got weird. What did she ask you?"

"That's super weird. She didn't ask me anything, she just told me that she had fun hanging out with all of us last night and that she'd like to do it again." Emma shrugged. Emma thought it was really weird that Karen had asked Kyle about her powers.

"Hmm. Damn it, Emma. Why'd you have to show her? Now, I might have to dump her weird ass."

"Oh, Kyle, don't break up with her. It's not every day you meet people who can do some of the shit I can. She's just curious. Just tell her to ask me next time. I love you two together and I don't want you dumping her 'cause of me."

"Well, if she starts to get any weirder I'm gonna have to. But you're right, I'm going to just blow it off. I do like her. Anyway, you at work tomorrow?"

"Yep, bright and early. I should be home later this afternoon. Wanna go get some sushi tonight?" Emma asked.

"Yeah, let's plan on it. Drive carefully. I'll talk to you later," Kyle said before hanging up.

Emma continued to drive down the highway. She began to wonder why Karen would question all these things. Maybe she, too, should give her the benefit of the doubt and shrug it off, but it was a little too weird.

***

As Emma arrived at the soccer field, she was surrounded by hundreds of players and scouts, as well as reporters. She couldn't believe how many players were here for what looked like tryouts. She couldn't see Mason right away, so she took a seat next to a few other ladies in the stands. They looked like they could be here for some of the soccer players, maybe their wives or girlfriends. As Emma searched the field for Mason, she started to listen in on the conversation.

"Tanner said that Jagger and Mason are the best guys to be signed to the team," the busty redhead stated.

"I'm really excited for this season. We have some really hot guys!" the blonde shrieked. "I really can't wait to meet Mason." She giggled.

Emma's blood pressure felt like it was boiling. She knew that it was more than possible for another guy to have the name Mason, but she couldn't help but think it was *her* Mason.

"His accent really makes my panties melt, but don't tell Tanner I said that," the redhead snickered. The two girls giggled and started to whisper to each other as Emma became more upset. Her mind went to the worst case scenario—Mason was going to do something with one of these girls.

She felt her powers building up, and rather than use them directly at the girls, she brought a ball flying in their direction, smacking the blonde in the side of her head. The redhead giggled, but quickly stopped to make sure her friend was okay. People all around the area were trying to figure out where the ball had come from. Emma snickered to herself and walked away.

"Emma!" Mason called out from one of the sidelines.

Emma blushed and waved as she walked toward him. "Hey," she greeted as she came closer. "I didn't think that it was going to be this busy. What's going on?"

"Tryouts. I basically have the position, but they want me to be out in front of reporters."

"Yeah, a few girls up there—they're really excited about you being here too." Emma glanced up to see the blonde holding her head, glaring at Emma.

"Ah, Tanner's girlfriend, Gia, and her friend, Lana. Them two birds are something else. Gia tried to hook me up with Lana last week, but after hearing her laugh and the way she talked down to everyone, I couldn't be bothered."

"Yeah, they are something," Emma agreed. "Apparently karma hit Lana. Literally." Emma laughed.

"I saw. Weirdest thing. I didn't see anyone kick the ball. Oh well. I'm glad you made it though."

"I'm glad I came. This is all really exciting!"

Mason stepped closer to Emma; he looked amazingly hot, all sweaty in his soccer gear. He grabbed Emma by the waist and kissed her softly. She could feel all the anger of the girls melt away.

As she slowly pulled away, she noticed a few of his teammates were watching and applauding Mason. He flipped them the bird and kissed Emma one more time.

"I've got to get back on the field, but stick around?"

Emma nodded and Mason raced back to a few of the other guys. Emma heard her phone vibrate in her purse. It was her mom calling. Emma smacked her forehead and quickly answered.

"Hey, Mom. I'm so sorry!"

"It's okay! How are things going?" Grace asked.

"They're…good! I haven't heard from my dad, which I don't know if that makes me nervous or happy. And I've been meeting up with this new guy."

"Honey, just be careful. I don't know why he's being so quiet lately. It makes me scared and I wish you would come home."

"Mom, I'm fine. I promise. I'm keeping my guard up and watching everything," Emma reassured her.

"Well, I have a little bit of news of my own," Grace said excitedly.

"Oh yeah?"

"Connor asked me to marry him!" Grace and Emma both shrieked.

"Oh my God, that's awesome! Congrats!" Emma cheered.

"Thank you! I'm on cloud nine…I've never been so happy. Well, the day you were born will never be topped."

"Aw, Mom, that's really sweet. I'm really happy

for the both of you! When are you having the wedding?"

"Oh we haven't really discussed that far out. It'll be something really small though. Do you think you'll be able to fly out here?"

"Of course! Just keep me posted. Hey, Mom, I gotta run. I'm at a soccer tryout and people are starting to cheer. I can't really hear you."

"All right, call me soon. I love you!" Grace shouted.

"Love you too!" Emma hollered, then disconnected. Emma took a seat as she realized Mason was playing. Watching him was incredible; he really was a great player. While waiting down on the end of the field, Mason glanced over at Emma, winking and blowing her a kiss. As she watched the game, her phone once again began to ring.

"Hello?" she answered.

"Do you think your new boyfriend will be able to save you? Better yet, do you think you can save him?" the cold voice said.

"Sebastian."

"Answer me, Emma. I mean, he plays a mean game of soccer and has taken your heart, but do you think it'll be enough?"

"Where are you?" Emma asked, looking all around the field.

"Don't bother looking for me. You won't see me. Now that you're without Micah backing you up, and your mother has gone home, do you think you can handle everything? All. Alone." Sebastian chuckled.

"I'm ready for you. You're really going to do

this in the middle of a soccer game?"

"Of course not. I like this little game. I'll see you soon, Emma." There was a click and the line went dead.

Emma hated the fact that he was playing cat and mouse with her. She still tried to search the entire place to see if she could see him sitting in the stands or standing on the field. Emma had no idea how he would know all this information. Maybe Micah was right, maybe he did have someone else and he was there watching. Emma's heart began to race. She was having a hard time concentrating on Mason.

"Miss, are you okay?" a reporter seated next to her asked.

Emma nodded. "I'm fine. I just feel a little light-headed."

He handed her a water bottle out of his bag. "Here, drink some water. You look really pale."

Emma took a few sips and felt the blood returning to her head. "Thank you," she whispered.

"Are you and Simmons an item?" he asked.

"Excuse me?"

"Mason Simmons," he stated, pointing to the field.

"Oh. Uh. I guess? I'm not sure what we really are yet. It's…you know, you're a reporter and I work for the newspaper, so I'm going to keep my mouth shut so it doesn't get turned around." Emma chuckled.

"Shit. You busted me. What paper do you work for?"

"I'm just a receptionist, but I work at Denver Press. Emma Blackwood." She introduced herself, shaking the guy's hand.

"Tom Gardner, Boulder Gazette. I thought I'd come down and get a big story." He chuckled. "Wait, Denver Press?"

Emma nodded. "Why?"

"Do you know a guy named Damon Ryder?"

Emma gasped. "Yeah. He used to work there. I guess he left while I was out of the office."

"He just applied with us and we might be taking him on. He a good guy?"

Emma didn't know what to say. Should she tell him the truth about their little fight or lie and say he was a great guy. He did seem like a hard worker— he had even worked really hard trying to get into her pants. "Yeah, hard worker. I was sad to hear he had left."

"Well, that's good to hear, maybe he'll get the job," Tom stated. "So, anything on or off the record you want to share?"

"Sorry, Tom, nothing. I hope you have fun though."

"Thanks, Emma. You too. I hope you feel better too."

Tom stood up and started to walk away. Emma looked at the water bottle and really hoped that this guy wasn't the guy hired to kill her and had just handed her a bottle of poison. So far she felt fine and nothing was happening. She let it go and made a mental note from now on not to take anything from random people while her dad was still out for vengeance.

Emma dumped the water bottle and sat back in her seat and continued to watch Mason and the rest of the players. She needed to keep all of her senses open to everything and everyone.

Chapter Ten

Once the practice had ended and the crowds began to thin, Emma made her way onto the field. Mason was speaking to someone who appeared to be one of the coaches. She didn't want to interrupt, but she thought it would be best to head home. Kyle was going to start to wonder where she was.

"Hiya, did you have fun?" Mason asked.

"That was amazing. I've never been to a soccer game. You guys run a lot!"

"Just a bit." He laughed. "You leaving?"

"I am. I promised Kyle to have some sushi with him and I need to get things done before work tomorrow as well. Call me later?" Emma asked, grabbing Mason's hand.

"Of course. What time do you get off tomorrow? The soccer team is doing a team dinner at seven."

"That sounds lovely. I should be off around five and then I'll have to go home and change. Casual dinner?"

"Actually…" he paused.

"Oh no, what?" Emma asked worriedly.

"It's a formal dinner," Mason stated.

"Oh no. Mason, I don't have anything formal to wear," Emma sulked.

"I'll take care of it." He winked.

Emma shook her head. "I can't let you do that!"

"I'm inviting you to a dinner that is formal dress, so yes, I will help. Just email this lady and let her know your size and the color," he insisted, pulling a card out of his jumper pocket. "She's taking care of my suit and she said if I needed anything to let her know."

"Are you sure?" Emma asked hesitantly.

"Yes. Go have fun with Kyle. I'm going to shower and rest. I'll ring you later."

Emma smiled widely. "Okay."

Mason kissed her and she turned to head out of the stadium. As she walked to the car, she suddenly remembered that she had asked Kyle to go with her to the car dealership after work. She hoped that he would understand if she postponed it one more day. As she approached the SUV she saw a tall male standing next to the car. Emma readied the alarm, but as she drew closer she realized she knew exactly who it was.

"What are you doing here?" she asked, crossing her arms.

"I see that me telling you that I love you and that I'm sorry meant absolutely nothing," Micah snapped.

"Micah…"

"I just wanted to make sure you're okay. I see that I shouldn't worry," he stated before starting to walk away.

"Micah, wait! What are you doing back here? Did you even leave? 'Cause I could've sworn I saw you talking to my dad the other day downtown!"

"I did leave. I got back this morning. I told you, Emma, I want nothing more to do with him. Why would I talk with him?" Micah asked, leaning up against the car next to hers.

"Why *are* you back?" Emma sighed.

"I got an email last night. Pictures of you and an attached note stating that I might want to say my goodbyes."

Emma's stomach flipped and she felt nauseous again. "He's coming for me? I mean, I'm ready, but I just…Micah, I hate this so much!"

"I know. This is really fucked up. Where are you going now?"

"I was heading home. Kyle and I are having dinner together and then I need to get ready for work in the morning." Emma felt like the entire world was closing in on her.

"Emma, breathe. You're going to pass out. Let's get you home," Micah insisted, helping her into the passenger seat.

"How am I going to get home if you're putting me in the passenger seat?"

"I'm going to drive you. Just lie back and catch your breath," Micah said as he closed her door and ran over to the driver's side. Emma placed her arm over her eyes as she tried to gain her composure. She knew she spoke too soon when she told her mom that things had been quiet. Micah sped down the highway and Emma soon started to doze off.

Before she knew it, Micah was parking in the

garage. Emma quickly sat up and hopped out. "Micah, I don't know how much Kyle is going to enjoy seeing you."

"I really don't care. I told you I'm here to make sure you're safe. I'll just come up and make sure you're fine and then I'll leave."

"Again?" Emma asked, her breath hitching.

"I'm in town for the rest of the week," he replied, trying to hide his smile.

"Well, I've got plans. Please try not to interfere. Please," Emma begged.

"I promise. Just know that I'm going to be around."

Emma nodded as they walked up the stairs of her building. Emma opened the door to Kyle blasting music and singing along. Karen was on the couch laughing at him. As Emma and Micah walked in, Kyle muted the music and he and Karen stared in shock as they walked in.

"What the fuck is he doing here?" Kyle shouted.

"Kyle, please, not right now."

"Em, what about Mason?" Karen asked.

"Look, he's here to make sure I got home okay. My dad called me and someone sent Micah an email saying he better come say his goodbyes. I'm getting nervous that things are going to start happening soon. I had a bit of a panic attack and Micah was nice enough to make sure I got home okay," Emma explained.

"Kyle, I know…" Micah started.

Kyle interrupted, "You don't know! Man, if Emma weren't standing right here and defending your ass, I'd fucking knock you out."

Micah laughed grimly. "Go ahead, I deserve it."

Kyle shook his head and walked away. Karen stood up and Micah gave her a look. Emma watched as Karen smirked and ran after Kyle into his room.

"What was that about?" Emma asked, confused.

"I don't know. You said that is Kyle's girlfriend, Karen?"

"Yeah. Look, I'm home. I'm fine. You might want to leave before anything else happens. Or Kyle actually decides that he is going to deck you."

"If you need me, I'm on my phone. I'm staying at the hotel just down the road. Call me, day or night. I'll be here in a minute."

Emma nodded as she walked Micah back to the door. He leaned in and kissed Emma's cheek and her heart felt like it stopped for that brief moment. "Bye, Micah."

Micah nodded and left her apartment. Emma locked the door and walked to Kyle's room. She could hear Karen and Kyle talking, but couldn't make out what they were saying. She softly knocked on the door. Karen opened the door with her purse in hand.

"I'll see ya later, Emma," Karen said as she rushed for the door.

"Karen? You okay?" Emma asked, trying to catch her. Karen slammed the door and Emma rushed into Kyle's room. "What happened?"

"She thought I should've knocked him out. Emma, as much as I despise the guy, he is always making sure you are safe. She was saying that I didn't defend her. I don't know. She's gone mental."

"I'm sorry. I shouldn't have let my dad get to me like that. I need to learn how to deal with some of the shit I hear. As weird as it is to hear, I'm ready for anything that's going to happen. Including being killed off. I don't know why, but I've come to terms with that."

"Emma, don't talk like that!" Kyle scolded. "All right, I need a drink. Let's go get dinner and a drink."

"Okay. Oh, so tomorrow, can we postpone the car thing. I was invited to go to a formal dinner with Mason." Emma beamed. At least this was something exciting to look forward to.

"Fancy. That's fine. Just let me know when."

Emma and Kyle walked out of the apartment and to the sushi place that was just around the corner from their building. She really could use some time with Kyle and take her mind off of everything that had just happened in the last couple of hours.

***

The rest of the night was enjoyed with sushi and Sake. Lots of Sake. Emma knew that Monday morning accompanied by a hangover was not a good combination, but she and Kyle were finally having a great time.

"Ky, I love you," Emma slurred.

"Love you too, Em. Why couldn't we have worked out?" Kyle asked as they stumbled up the stairs to their apartment.

"'Cause it was too weird. We were just better off as friends. That and I recall you liked my friend,

Nicki, and I think you were just hanging with me to get to her."

"That's not true, Em. I really did like you, but like you said, I think we acted more like siblings than lovers." Kyle helped Emma onto the couch, where she lay down and snuggled into a blanket. "Are you going in to work tomorrow?" he asked, taking Emma's shoes off.

"Ugh, yeah. I might need extra coffee though."

"All right, I'm gonna call it a night. See ya in the morning." Kyle stumbled to his bedroom and Emma realized she had to still make it to her bed.

As she pushed herself off the couch, she stumbled onto the floor. Her phone began to vibrate in her pocket, causing her to jump. It was Micah.

"Micah, I'm a little too drunk to have any sort of conversation," she stated, answering the phone.

"It's Ying," he said quietly

Emma felt like she sobered up immediately. "What's wrong?" she panicked.

"I need your help. Can I come get you?"

"Y-yeah. When will you be here?" she stuttered, looking for her keys.

"I'm on my way. I should be there in five minutes," he said, disconnecting the line. Emma didn't know if she should go tell Kyle and have him worry or just leave. She tried to scribble a note on the fridge—hopefully she'd be home way before he saw it.

She quietly opened the door and locked it behind her. She ran down the stairs and raced out the door to find Micah pulling up to the curb.

"What happened?" Emma asked, pulling herself

into the SUV.

"Your dad…" he began. She'd never seen Micah look so distraught and it broke her heart. "I guess he went to see her. She sent me a message saying he just showed up and that I needed to get over there. I rushed over there as fast as I could, but I was too late."

"Did he…" Emma sniffed.

"No, but I'm pretty sure he took her powers from her."

"Micah, I didn't think this was possible! My mom said that he couldn't do it unless he was really strong," Emma stated, confused.

"He can't take them for himself, but he can hurt someone and take their powers. I need you to just help her. She needs to be healed as much as possible."

"Micah…I-I…"

"You can. This is your chance to be tested for real. He's getting to the point of hurting people around you, Emma. He's not going to keep playing these games. He's going to get impatient and he's going to come for you next."

Emma nodded her head and sat back in the seat. Her heart was racing ninety miles per hour. As Micah sped down the highway, she began to nod off.

***

"Emma, you see what I'm capable of. Why don't you just give up?" Sebastian asked, sitting across from her on a couch.

"Because I won't let you win. I won't let you hurt any more people. You need to go away, Sebastian. Far, far away."

"As your father, maybe I'm willing to let things work out and you can just help me become stronger. There are so many people with powers out there and they need someone to rule over them…"

"Sebastian, you're sick. Just stop. Go away!"

***

"Emma? We're here," Micah said softly, gently shaking her.

"Sorry," Emma said, rubbing her eyes. With Micah's help she stepped out of the SUV and walked up to the entrance of the jewelry store. Micah led her into the back room, where Ying was laying on the little bed in the corner. She looked like she was in pain. "Micah, are you sure she doesn't need a doctor?"

"This is a curse. Nothing a doctor is going to be able to fix. They'd probably think it was food poisoning." Micah walked over to Ying's side and held her hand. "Ying, Emma's here. She's gonna help, okay? Just hold on."

"Micah, I don't think I can get her powers back," Emma said, walking over to Ying.

"I know." He sighed. "We just need to get her better. She can really help you with your dad."

"How? She doesn't have any powers!" Emma was so confused by everything that was happening.

"Emma," Ying whispered. "Please help me."

Emma nodded and placed her hands on Ying,

closing her eyes. She took a deep breath and prayed that she was strong enough to help someone who was cursed. Emma could feel her powers at her fingertips, and the power between her fingers and Ying's body felt so strong. Emma could feel a force trying to fight Emma's powers off.

"Emma, don't break that connection. You have the curse in your hands. You just need to make it disappear," Micah whispered.

"I don't know how!" Emma said exhaustedly. She felt like this was draining her.

"Use your dark magic to make it go." Micah placed his hand on her back. Emma nodded and channeled her dark powers. She immediately felt stronger, felt more powerful against this force. She could see the color returning to Ying's face.

Ying coughed and slowly sat up. "Emma, you did it," she whispered. "You really are very strong. Now, kill the bastard."

Emma sighed and sat down on the bed. "I don't know how."

"You're going to need a little help. You have so much power, but your body is not as strong." Ying stood up and walked over to an end table. She grabbed a gold chain with a pendant attached. "Wear this. I promise it's nothing like the bracelet. It will help bring your body the strength you need."

Emma slipped the necklace over her head and hoped that this would really help. If she felt drained just healing someone, she was never going to be able to keep her life against her father.

"I really should head back. I've got to get to work early in the morning. Micah, can you please take me home?"

Micah nodded as Ying gave Emma a hug. "Emma, I can't thank you enough. If you need anything, please come see me," Ying whispered in her ear.

Emma felt a tear fall down her face as she nodded into Ying's shoulder. Micah led Emma back to the SUV and helped her into the passenger seat. The whole drive to Emma's apartment was a silent one. Emma examined the pendant, a Celtic knot with a purple fluorite crystal in the middle.

"Fluorite helps with healing," Micah stated as he pulled up to her apartment. Emma tucked the pendant into her top and reached for the door. Micah grabbed her arm and she quickly turned to him and pressed her lips hard into his. His arms pulled her over the console and up against his hard body. It felt so good to be in his arms again.

Emma's thoughts were racing and the thought of Mason popped into her head. "Micah," she said, trying to pull away. "I...I can't."

Micah nodded as Emma quickly exited the SUV. She ran upstairs and into her bedroom. She felt the butterflies swarming in her stomach. She couldn't believe she was just kissing Micah. Tomorrow couldn't come soon enough.

Chapter Eleven

Emma's alarm went off at six thirty and she felt the pain of the Sake from the night before and hoped that everything after dinner with Kyle had been a dream. Until she felt the necklace around her neck. She sighed as she padded to the bathroom.

When she finished getting ready, she walked out to see Kyle making some coffee. "Morning," she said, rubbing her temple.

"Whose idea was it to have so much Sake?" Kyle grumbled.

"Yours, I think." She giggled.

"No more. What time is your dinner function tonight?" he asked, pulling two travel mugs from the cabinet.

"Oh shit! I forgot to email this woman about my dress!" Emma gasped, running to grab her phone from her room. She pulled the card out of her capris pocket and quickly typed out an email, giving her all the information Mason had told her to give. She pressed *send*, hoping that she wasn't too late and that the woman could help her.

"Emma? What's this note about you leaving with Micah?" Kyle asked, pointing to the chicken scratch on the fridge note board.

"It's a really weird story…" Emma started as she cleared her throat. "Let me get some coffee and I can explain."

"Look, I'm not your dad, obviously, so let's just say parent. I'm not your parent or your keeper, but with all this crazy shit, just come tell me that you're leaving. I might convince you to stay, but I want you to be safe."

"Thanks, Kyle. It was kind of an emergency and I had to leave. I didn't want to worry you and, unfortunately, I didn't have time to be convinced to stay. I had to go help Ying. I promise I will let you know next time."

Kyle walked up to Emma and gave her a hug. "I'm just worried that I'm going to lose you. I don't have many friends, Em, I just want to keep you around for a little bit. And even though you suck at paying your half of the rent, it still helps," he joked.

"Shut up. I promise I will be fine. You're not going to lose me," Emma reassured him. "Now, get me some coffee and let's go to work." Emma laughed.

Kyle filled both mugs and grabbed his laptop bag before he and Emma headed out the door. It was going to be nice to get back to work and not let the memories of the last few weeks be a constant nagging in the back of her head.

On the way to the office, Kyle filled Emma in on the new staff and how Phil and his wife finally filed divorce papers. Phil had been worried that his wife was going to take him for everything he had, but in the end walked away happy. Kyle said now that he was done with the whole divorce, he was actually more pleasant to work with. Then he went on to talk about Paula. "She's really sweet and she'll be helping you a lot. It's been a lot busier with the warmer weather and more news coming through," he stated, pulling into the parking lot.

"So, am I sharing a desk with her?" Emma asked as she stepped out of the SUV.

"No, she's around the corner, but she'll be helping you answer the phone lines. You might really get along with her."

Kyle held the door open for Emma and they were greeted by a young woman with long brown hair. Even behind her glasses you could see her sparkling blue eyes. She stood up, smiling brightly. "Morning, Kyle! How was your weekend?"

"Hi, Paula. It was nice, thanks. Paula, this is Emma."

"Oh! Hi! I've heard so many nice things about you! I can't wait to work with you!" she said enthusiastically.

"Hi, Paula. I've heard nice things about you as well." Emma walked around to her desk and set her things down. "I'm gonna go fill up my coffee mug. Paula, can I get you anything?"

"No, I'm good, thanks. I'm going to move my things back to my desk. See ya in a bit."

Emma walked back to the breakroom and filled her coffee mug with warm coffee and some of the nice cream. Kyle liked his coffee black at home, and most the time so did Emma, but she found that she really enjoyed the creamer that the office kept stocked. As she returned she saw Paula speaking to Mason. She was in shock to see him standing in her workplace.

"Hey! What are you doing here?" Emma asked excitedly, walking up to Mason and giving him a tight hug.

"I thought I'd bring you this." He held up a Styrofoam box.

"What is it?" Emma asked, taking it from him.

"Breakfast. It's from the crepe place. I figured you could use a nice meal on your first day back from a vacation."

Emma smiled widely. "Mason, that is really sweet! Thank you." Paula sighed and Emma turned and giggled at her. "Paula, this is Mason."

"I'm her boyfriend," Mason added. Emma blushed as the two shook hands.

"Very nice to meet you," Paula stated.

"Well, I should head back. I got a call from the lady about a tux fitting. She mentioned she received your email and will have a few dresses brought to you this afternoon. I'll pick you up from your place about half past six, okay?"

"Sounds great. Thank you again for breakfast." Emma gave him a soft kiss and he headed out of the building.

"Oh my God! He is so hot, Emma!" Paula gushed.

"Thanks. He really is like a god. I really don't know how I am getting so lucky with these hot guys!" Emma joked.

"Well, I'm going to have to hang out with you

more often so I can take one of them off your hands." Paula laughed.

"Paula, you don't have to leave the front desk, I'm sure we can share it—that way you can fill me in on the office gossip that Kyle doesn't have access to."

"Thanks, I'd love to gossip."

As Emma and Paula situated their desk items, a flower delivery man walked in with a large bouquet. "I have a delivery for Emma Blackwood," he stated, placing the vase on the edge of the desk.

"That's me, but who are they from?" she asked, looking for the card.

"If that sexy man sent you flowers too, I'm going to get super jealous," Paula said as she signed the board for Emma.

Emma pulled the card and found a message.

Welcome back to work, Emma. The time is coming.
-Dad.

Emma tossed the card in the flowers and grabbed the vase. "Excuse me!" she shouted at the delivery man. "I'd like these to go back."

"I'm sorry, what?" the driver asked, confused.

"Take them back. Tell the sender to leave me alone!" Emma shoved the vase back at the man and stormed off before he could get her to change her mind.

"Emma, is everything okay? Were they not from Mason?" Paula asked.

"No. And if we receive anything else for me that

is from a Sebastian Blackwood, please return it."

"All right," Paula said quietly.

"I'll tell you about it later. Right now, I just want to get to work," Emma said solemnly. She felt bad, her first day back and she was already having drama and was taking it out on Paula. "I'm sorry, Paula. I didn't mean to snap. Make it up to you with lunch?"

Paula nodded and smiled. Emma buried herself in the paperwork and made sure to answer all the phone calls to keep herself busy until lunch.

*****

Once lunchtime rolled around, Emma and Paula escaped to a little Mexican restaurant down the block. Emma filled Paula in on some of the drama she was dealing with, without going into too much depth. She told her that her dad was somewhat crazy and wanted to reunite with her and she wanted nothing to do with him. Paula agreed not to allow anything in the building from him and told her she would call the delivery services. Emma continued on to the Micah situation and just said he was an ex who might show up from time to time and she might have to leave.

"Wow, you really do have man problems," Paula joked.

"You have *no* idea. I promise that I won't let it get too out of hand. I should have it under control really soon."

"Not a problem. Ever since Phil and his wife made their divorce official, he's been totally relaxed. So I don't think it will be a problem," Paula reassured her.

"Thanks. You know, I was worried that I wasn't going to be able to fit back in after leaving and you helping out, but now I'm so glad that we could be deskmates." Emma smiled.

"Me too. I was thinking that I was going to have to go back to the accounting dungeon once you got back. I enjoy being out in the open." Paula laughed.

The girls finished up their meals and headed back to the office. They realized they had been gone for almost an hour and a half so they quickly got back to work before Phil's 'relaxed attitude' went away. As Emma sat down, a woman with red, curly hair walked in through the door, carrying a garment bag over her shoulder.

"Hi, can I help you?" Emma asked, standing.

"I'm Charisse. I'm looking for Emma Blackwood. I have her dresses." Charisse hung the bag on the coat hanger stand that was standing next to the desk.

"Oh, I'm Emma! Thank you so much! Do I pay with a card or check?" Emma asked hesitantly.

She chuckled. "They are taken care of. I picked out three dresses for you, so you have some starter dresses. I hope you don't mind, besides the black, I got you a red and a purple. If you need anything else, please call or email me," she stated, walking away.

"Thank you," Emma called out. She picked up the garment bag off the hanger and shrieked. "Do you mind if I go try these on really fast?" Emma asked Paula.

"No! I want to see!" Paula exclaimed as Emma

ran to the bathroom. Kyle watched as she ran by and quickly followed.

"Emma?" Kyle asked, opening the door.

"Kyle!" Emma screeched, covering her chest as he opened the door.

"Oh shit! I'm sorry, I thought something was wrong!"

"Close the door! I'm trying to dress!"

Kyle shut the door, embarrassed. Emma quickly tried on the long, black gown. She immediately beamed when she saw herself in the mirror. She opened the door to see a blushing Kyle standing there. His eyes widened as he saw Emma step out of the bathroom.

"Damn, Em, you look…hot!" he said.

"Thanks, Kyle. It's not too…tight?" she asked, smoothing out the dress.

"No. Not at all."

"Emma! I love it!" Paula exclaimed as she walked toward her. "Is that the one you're going to wear tonight?"

"I didn't try on the others, but I think so." Emma beamed as she turned back for the bathroom. She was extremely excited to wear this dress tonight. So much so that she didn't even want to take it off so she could get back to work. She looked at herself several more times in the mirror before she took it off. Now she only had to figure out how to wear her hair.

Once Emma got back to work, the day seemed to drag on. She couldn't wait to see Mason and wear her gown.

"Denver Press, this is Paula." Emma heard Paula

answer the phone. She must have had her head in the clouds because she didn't even hear the phone ring. "Yes, she's right here." Paula placed the phone on hold. "Emma…" she started hesitantly. "Your mom is on the phone and she sounds upset."

"Mom?" Emma quickly answered.

"I'm just making sure you're okay. I got a phone call today from Ying. She said you saved her life. Honey, I think that you should lay low for a while."

"Mom, I just got back from laying low. I really need to get out and…Mom, I'm at work and I'm surrounded by people. He told me that he wouldn't do it front of people. Please just stop worrying," Emma snapped.

"Honey…"

"No, I don't want you to worry! Please, just plan the wedding with Connor. I'm fine. I'll handle this on my own!"

The phone went dead. Emma stared at the receiver, feeling a little bad she snapped at her mom like that. She knew that she meant well, and it was her mom after all, but she was so sick of everyone treating her like a fragile doll.

"Everything okay?" Paula asked cautiously.

"Yeah, just family drama." Emma wished that it was a lie, but it really was family drama. One that she wished would just go away.

"Well, it's quarter to four, why don't you head out and get ready!" Paula suggested.

"Really? Are you sure?" Emma asked.

"Of course! I want a full report of how it went tomorrow!" she screeched, winking at Emma.

"You've got it!" Emma gathered her things and

grabbed the dresses off the hanger. She ran to Kyle's desk and bobbed up and down.

"Hey, I'm gonna head out. I'll catch a cab, okay?"

"Nah, just take my car. I'll catch a ride home with Karen. We were talking about going to dinner." Just then his phone beeped. "Never mind on dinner, she had to fly home. She seriously has been acting weird. Just take the car; I don't want you having to take a cab."

"Wow, Kyle, you're kinda turning into a softie lately." Emma chuckled.

"Yeah, yeah, yeah. All right, I'll see you later. Call me if you need anything."

Emma nodded and dashed out of the office. She was getting more and more excited, but there was a lingering feeling that something was going to happen. She picked up her phone and couldn't believe she was about to call the one person she knew would have somewhat of a clue.

"Are you okay?" Micah answered.

"Yes, I'm fine! I just want…God, I feel so weird asking you this, but I'm going to a formal banquet tonight and there is just a lingering feeling something is going on."

"I've been having that feeling too. Have you heard from him?"

Emma sighed. "He sent me flowers this morning. Micah, I've been calm about this whole thing, but now I'm getting to the point where I'm a little scared. Like something is going to happen to someone I love. I really have come to terms with it being me he wants, but I don't think I could handle it if he hurt Kyle or my mom." Emma could feel the tears piercing her lids.

"I know," he whispered.

"Can you just do me a favor? Can you keep an eye on Kyle? I know he doesn't like you much, and you can't stand him, but I just need to know that he's okay," Emma pleaded. Micah stayed silent for a moment. "Micah? Are you still there?"

"Yeah." He paused. "I'll keep an eye on him. You're the one I'm worried about, though."

"I know you are. I appreciate it, but just for tonight. I don't want to have to worry about him."

"All right, be careful," he insisted.

Emma smiled, wishing Micah could've been this way when they were together. "I will. I'll have my phone, so call me if anything happens."

"Emma…" Micah started.

"Yeah?" Her stomach began to tense up.

"Nothing. I'll talk to you later. Have fun." Micah disconnected the call and Emma started the car. She figured that since she waited this long to go, she might as well ask Kyle if he wanted to just come home with her. She dialed his number.

"Hey, I got a phone call and haven't left yet. Do you need a ride?" Emma asked when Kyle picked up.

"Yeah, I'm walking out now. See ya in a second," Kyle stated, walking around the corner. As much as she was excited to go tonight, she was now wishing she could keep everyone she loved with her at all times.

Chapter Twelve

"Ugh! Why won't my hair stay up?" Emma shouted at her reflection. She had been struggling to figure out how to wear her hair since she had gotten home.

"Em, Mason's here!" Kyle hollered, poking his head into her room.

"I'll be there in just a second," she said, pinning her hair into place. She smoothed the long black gown out and walked into the living room. Mason was standing in the hallway, wearing his tux. Emma smiled widely. "Wow. You look…amazing."

"You know, I'm supposed to tell you that." Mason chuckled. "Ready?"

Emma nodded and walked up to Kyle, hugging him. "I have a bad feeling about tonight, so please stay in, okay?" she whispered in his ear. He pulled away, giving her a confused look.

"Should you go, then?" he asked, looking at Mason.

"I'll be fine. Just be careful."

Emma walked up to Mason. "Let's go," she said,

smiling. As they walked out the front door, Emma felt a sharp pain in her side.

"Are you all right?" Mason asked as she groaned, grabbing her side.

"I'm fine," she lied. "I'm really excited about tonight."

"Me too. I can't wait to show you off," he stated. They walked down the stairs to see a limo waiting for them at the curb. Mason helped her into the back and the driver shut the door behind Mason. "Hungry?"

"*Starving*." Emma laughed.

Mason laced his fingers with Emma's. "You really do look beautiful."

Emma blushed. "Thank you."

The car started to slow. Emma realized they were at the convention center. There were several cameras at the front doors. Her heart began to race as she noticed the massive amount of people all around and couldn't make out every face. The pain in her side became a little stronger. Mason reached for her hand and she walked cautiously toward the entrance of the building. Suddenly, someone grabbed her arm. Her whole body tensed as she gasped.

"Emma!"

She turned to see who was grabbing her arm. She looked up to see Damon standing behind her.

"Damon?" she said nervously.

"Hey! I thought that was you! How are you?" he asked, pulling her into a hug. She was relieved that he didn't remember anything that had happened between them.

"Hi, Damon, you look well." Emma looked to see Mason waiting by the doors for her.

"I am, thanks. Sorry that I didn't get to see you before I left the paper. I had a job opportunity come up and I needed to take it. So, what are you doing here?" he asked.

"I'm here with one of the players, Mason Simmons," Emma responded, pointing to Mason.

"Wow, that's great! Well, I gotta get back to work. If you have time, give me a call. We'll do coffee or lunch," he insisted, handing her a business card. Emma slipped it in her purse and nodded. Damon turned and met up with another reporter and Emma turned to hurry toward Mason.

"Friend?" Mason asked curiously.

"Yeah, well, he used to work with me. Sorry."

"No worries. Let's head in." Mason opened the door for Emma as they walked in. Emma realized that this was not just for his team, but for every major team in Colorado. She suddenly became intimidated by all of the celebrities who were mingling.

"Holy shit, Mason, you didn't tell me this was a big to-do," she whispered, gripping his hand.

"Sorry, love, I didn't think that it was going to be all the teams. Can I get you a drink?" he asked as they walked toward the bar.

Emma nodded. She was going to need a lot to drink to get through the night. The pain in her side was starting to disappear. She didn't know if that was a good sign or if it was a sign of worse things to come.

Mason got her a glass of champagne and they

walked into the dining room to find their seats. Emma sat down as Mason excused himself to go speak to a few of his teammates. Emma pulled out her phone to see if she had any messages. To her relief there were none. As she placed it back in her bag, it vibrated. Her heart stopped.

Kyle: I'm bored. I think I'm going to head to Matchboxes. I need to get a hot chick and fast!

Emma sighed as she read Kyle's message. She couldn't help but feel responsible for the way Karen was acting. This was the first girl that Kyle had ever been serious about and she was actually blowing him off.

Emma: Just make sure you are careful. Don't sleep with anyone yet. I'm sure Karen will snap out of it.

Mason returned to the table with three other men. "Emma, I'd like you to meet some of the guys," he stated, helping Emma stand. "Guys, this is my girlfriend, Emma." Mason smiled widely. Emma couldn't help but feel giddy at the way he introduced her as his girlfriend.

***

Emma and Mason spent the rest of the night mingling with sports stars and their spouses. She had never felt so fancy. As the time rolled around to eleven, Emma yawned, sitting at the table.

121

"Are you ready to leave?" Mason asked, rubbing her arm.

"I'm sorry, you probably need to stay, huh?" Emma asked, masking her yawn.

"No, let's get you home. I'd also like to get you out of this dress." He winked.

Emma giggled as she grabbed her purse. She checked her phone for the millionth time that night. She hadn't heard back from Kyle since he said he was leaving, and she couldn't help but worry the rest of the night. If something had happened, she was sure Micah would let her know.

Mason escorted Emma out to the limo and helped her slide in. Emma snuggled into Mason's side as the driver took off down the road. She, too, couldn't wait for him to help her out of the dress. She had been watching him all night in his tux and couldn't believe how hot he looked in it.

Once they arrived at her apartment, she could feel the sexual tension building between them. Before she could unlock the door, Mason pushed her against the wall and pressed his lips hard into hers. His hands explored up and down her hips and breasts.

"I wanted to rip this thing off you in that limo, but it wasn't a long enough drive." He breathed heavily against her.

"Let's get inside before my neighbors call the police." Emma giggled, opening the door. Once inside, Emma could hear two men laughing at the loud television. Emma peeked around the corner and saw Micah and Kyle watching TV.

"Oh hey, Em!" Kyle slurred. "Micah showed up

at Matchboxes and we had a couple of beers and cleared the air."

Emma glared at Micah, who didn't have anything to say. "Well…" Emma seethed. "Micah, I think that you should leave."

"No, he's my buddy now!" Kyle shouted, trying to stand up. He had obviously had more than a couple of beers.

"No, it's okay. I'm going to leave," Micah said quietly as he noticed Mason standing in the hallway.

"All right, man, well, next week it's my treat and we'll find you some hot chick!" Kyle laughed.

"Bye, Micah," Emma said. Micah nodded as he walked by Mason and Emma to the front door. Emma glared at Kyle as he stumbled to his bedroom. Emma grabbed Mason's hand and led him to her room. "I'm so sorry, Mason."

"I'm a bit confused. Who is Micah?" he asked as he closed the door behind him.

"He's…he's my ex," Emma stated. Mason nodded his head once and took a seat on the edge of the bed. Emma felt really embarrassed. "We broke up a little bit ago."

"Well…" Mason began. Emma was a little nervous that he was going to be upset. "His loss."

Emma looked at him, puzzled. "His loss?"

"He let a beautiful, wonderful, amazing woman get away, and now I get her," he stated, pulling her close to him. He began to unzip her dress and lowered it to the floor. He kissed her stomach. Emma pushed him back onto the bed and straddled him.

"You're pretty great too," she whispered. "I'm pretty excited that I get you."

Mason rolled over to get Emma onto her back. "I need to use the toilet. Don't you move an inch," he insisted as he got up and unbuttoned his shirt.

Emma watched him walk into her bathroom and shut the door. She pulled the pins out of her hair and placed them on the table next to her, then snapped her fingers, lighting the candles around the room. She ran her fingers through her hair and caught a glimpse of her makeup in the mirror on her dresser.

Mason returned to the bedroom and noticed the candles were lit. He gave Emma a look. "I thought I told you not to move," he joked.

Emma chuckled, knowing she really didn't leave the bed. "I know, but I couldn't resist."

Mason returned to her on the bed, softly kissing her lips. With every soft, passionate kiss, Emma enjoyed being with Mason, but couldn't help have her mind wander back to Micah. She almost felt incredibly guilty.

Chapter Thirteen

"Good morning, beautiful," Mason whispered. They had spent almost the entire night making love. She finally got out of her own head, cleared any thoughts of Micah, and enjoyed her time with Mason. If she could get Micah away, she could actually see things becoming something long-term with Mason. She really did like him.

"Morning," she responded, smiling. "What time is it?"

"Almost six. You have to work today?" he asked, trailing his finger down her back. He then grabbed the pendant that was laying next to her head on the pillow, examining it. "This is nice."

"Yeah, unfortunately I do have to work. Thanks, a dear friend gave it to me," she said, looking down at the pendant.

Mason nodded and gently placed it back on the bed. "Plans tonight?"

Emma nodded into the pillow, enjoying the tickling sensation on her back. "I'm actually going to be a grown up and get a car." She giggled.

"Right, well, I'd like to see you very soon," Mason stated, kissing the top of her head.

"I have the rest of the week free."

"Good. You're all mine," he stated, pushing himself out of bed. "I'd like to take you for a ride on my motorbike too."

"You have a motorcycle?" Emma asked excitedly. She had always wanted to go for a ride on one.

"By the excitement in your voice, I know exactly what I'm doing with you all weekend. We'll have a laugh and go for a long ride. Ah shite!"

"Mason? You okay?" Emma asked, sitting up.

"I forgot I have practice this week and a game on Thursday night. So, how about we plan for us to spend the weekend together?"

Emma smirked. "I'd love that."

"I'm going to miss seeing you, though," he said, leaning in and kissing her softly on the lips.

"It's only a few days. I'll see you on Friday."

Mason stood up and slipped on his clothes. "Do you want to go? To the game that is."

"That sounds like fun. Maybe Kyle and I can go."

"I'll have them place some tickets at the box office. I've got to run, love, but I'll call you later. Have a great day at work."

Emma waved goodbye as she realized she needed to get ready. Could she already be having feelings for this man? "Too soon, Emma," she whispered to herself.

"Emma? You up?" Kyle asked, knocking on her door.

"Yeah. I hope that Mason leaving didn't wake you," she said, slipping her robe on before opening her door.

"No, I woke up in dire need of water. I haven't drank that much in a long time. Sorry if we pissed you off."

"Not pissed, just was a little awkward having him here. You guys are besties now?" Emma joked.

Kyle rubbed his head. "It's too early to be a dick." He chuckled. "He's actually pretty decent to hang out with. But you told him to babysit me?"

"What?" Emma screeched.

"I saw him as I was leaving and then he pulled into the parking lot behind me. At first I wasn't too keen on seeing him, but he told me that your dad is fucking with you. Why didn't you tell me?"

"I didn't want you to worry, Kyle. You've got Karen drama and work. I just didn't want to add one more thing to your plate."

"Emma, no matter what shit I have going on, I'm still gonna worry about you! Besides, I think drama with Karen is over. I told her we should think about taking a break and she never responded, so it's all good."

"I'm so sorry," Emma said, hugging Kyle. "Maybe she's just busy with her family. I'm sure it will work out. You guys were, like, made for each other."

"Fuck it. Well, I gotta get in the shower. You should too. You smell like sex and it's kinda pissing me off," he joked.

"Shut up! I don't smell like sex…do I?" Emma backed away from Kyle.

"No, but I'm not dumb. Anyway, car tonight?"

Emma nodded excitedly. "Yes!"

"I'm gonna shower and make coffee. See ya in a few." Kyle trudged down the hallway and Emma's phone began to vibrate.

"Hello?" she answered.

"Emma, dear, I'm mad that you didn't appreciate my flowers," Sebastian snapped.

"Are you serious?"

"I'm so sick of being nice! Get ready, Emma. The time is here. I'm sick of giving you time, so you could at least die trying, but now I'm done." The phone line disconnected and Emma began to sob. She set her phone down and balled up on her bed. She wished that this was all a dream and would just go away. She was ready to wake up and for everything to be normal.

Wiping her tears, she pushed any sort of hurt or scared emotions to the back and wanted to bring out the hate and anger. She sat up, took a deep breath, and felt all of her dark powers at her fingertips. She wasn't going to let him hurt her or anyone. Ever.

***

Emma stepped out of her room after she was finished readying herself for work. Kyle was leaning up against the fridge.

"Kyle? You okay?" Emma asked, rushing to his side.

"Yeah, just hungover," he said with a laugh. He pushed himself up and grabbed the coffee pot, only to notice there was no coffee in it. "Jesus, I forgot to turn this on!" Kyle grumbled.

"I'll drive just to be on the safe side, then." Emma looked at her watch. "Come on, we'll stop and get some coffee before work."

Emma and Kyle grabbed their things and headed out the door. Emma looked everywhere as they walked into the parking lot. More than ever, she felt paranoid. As she got in the car, she held up her hands and began to recite a spell she remembered reading about protecting people. She really hoped that the necklace would help her, but this spell would keep Kyle safe.

"Em, what are you doing?" Kyle hollered in the car.

"Nothing. I'm just making sure I have everything," she lied. She knew that Kyle wanted to be informed of everything that was going on, but she couldn't bring herself to do that now. "Ready?"

"Coffee…"

"Yes, I know. We're going." Emma laughed.

Emma was tempted to stop at her old job, but playing catch up with Casey was not something she was willing to do this morning. She knew how much he hated the morning shifts and it wasn't worth it. She pulled in through the closest McDonald's drive-through and ordered their coffee. She ordered Phil and Paula some coffee as well and sped into work.

"Remind me to talk you out of any car that goes fast." Kyle breathed heavily as he got out of the car.

"What? Why?" Emma asked, shocked.

"'Cause, dude, you fucking drove Mach five all the way here. I'm surprised we didn't get a ticket!"

"Oh my God! I wasn't going that fast. Get your ass into work." Emma chuckled. She took the drink holder from Kyle and carried it into the office. Paula greeted them both with her million-dollar smile. "Morning! I brought coffee!" Emma said cheerily. Paula clapped as Emma placed the cup on her desk and took the other cup into Phil's office. "Morning, Phil. I brought you some coffee."

"Morning, Emma. I'm glad that you're in here. Can you shut the door?" Phil asked seriously.

Emma quietly shut the door and took a seat in front of his desk. "Am I in trouble?" she nervously asked.

He picked up a competitor's newspaper off his desk and pointed out a picture of her and Mason on one of the pages. "I wish you would have informed me that you were going to this dinner."

"Phil, I'm sorry. I didn't know that…"

"I tried to get a couple of our columnists out there, but either they couldn't get on the list or were tied up. I could've used someone to cover it."

"Phil, I'm not a writer. I actually suck at writing," Emma huffed. "Besides, I was a guest. I don't think they would have appreciated me asking questions."

"Emma, if you're going to be attending more of these functions, I want you to take a notebook and pen. I know you're not a writer, but we can get Kyle to clean it up or you can take him with you." Phil tossed the paper back onto his desk. "I'm officially going to give you a raise to be our inside reporter."

"Phil…I don't know…" Emma began.

"Here's a press pass. I'm sure you can get on the

record. H.R. has already been notified and increased your salary. You can still be front desk, but when you leave and are into anything exclusive—I want it covered. Thanks again for the coffee."

Emma stood up and looked at her new ID badge. "Uh, thanks," she said quietly before leaving. She walked over to Kyle's desk. "I have *no* idea what the hell just went on," she said, showing him the badge.

"Wow. Since when are you going to be doing stories?" Kyle asked, amused.

"Apparently since I'm dating Mason. I'm not going to be able to get anything! This is a fucking crazy day." Emma sat down on the chair next to his desk and sighed. "Kyle, why can't things ever be…normal?"

"'Cause you aren't normal, Em. Look, all you have to do is cover events. It's not like you have to interview anyone. If you're going to another fancy dinner, write about who was there, why it was happening, and the location and all the other shit. I'll fluff it up and make it sound nice and it'll be done."

"Thanks, Ky. All right, I'm gonna get back to work. I'll see you later." Emma stood up and Kyle gave her a nod before she walked back to her desk.

"Hi, how was last night?" Paula asked. It looked like it was killing her to wait to hear all the details. Emma giggled as she began to recall the evening.

"Where do I begin?" Emma started, taking a sip of her coffee.

Chapter Fourteen

Emma and Paula spent most of the day gossiping about last night's function. Emma felt like she was a star to Paula. She was really glad she had someone to talk to, but she really wished that Karen was around too. She would've enjoyed hearing it. During lunch she decided to call her mom; she knew that she had been kind of rude with her the other day and her mom deserved an apology. She took her cell phone outside and sat on the bench.

She called her mom's phone, but it went straight to voice mail. Emma felt a little hurt that her mom had turned off her phone. "Hey, Mom, it's me. I…I wanted to apologize for the way I was the other day. You didn't deserve that attitude. I love you tons and I want to tell you some cool news that's been happening. So give me a call and…I'll talk to you later. Love ya."

Emma hung her phone up and walked back to her desk and buried herself in work. Paula had to leave early for a doctor's appointment, so she was all alone the rest of the day.

"Wow, today went by fast," Kyle stated, walking up to Emma's desk. "Ready to go?"

"Yep, lemme just shut this down and we can go."

"So, what kind of car are you getting?" he asked, handing Emma her purse that was on the edge of the desk.

"I want a Jeep, like yours," she stated excitedly.

"Good choice. We can go talk to Logan down at the dealership. He can hook you up with a good deal."

Emma and Kyle headed down to the dealership and looked around. Emma fell in love with a bright red Jeep Grand Cherokee. Kyle and Logan, a younger-looking man, had chatted over everything while Emma looked around the lot to see if anything else screamed her name, but she was hooked. Kyle brought the price down a bit and Emma signed the paperwork. She was officially a car owner and now felt like everything was going great. As Logan handed her the keys, the pain in Emma's side caused her to double over.

"Kyle, is your friend okay?" Logan asked as he watched Kyle help her to a chair.

Emma nodded as she took a deep breath in. "I'm fine…I just get these pains from time to time."

"Can you get her some water?" Kyle asked Logan. As Logan walked away, Kyle squatted down to look at Emma. "What's going on?"

"He's around here," she whispered.

"Who?" he asked, looking around the dealership.

"My dad. He told me that the time is coming. I don't know when, but I've been feeling this pain and I know he's around here."

"Emma!" Kyle exclaimed as Logan brought over a paper cup filled with water.

"Thank you, Logan." Emma took all the water in her mouth and stood up. "Let's head out."

Logan nodded and handed her the keys to her new car. She walked got in and excitedly adjusted the seat, trying to ignore the nagging pain. She knew she didn't have a choice but to talk more about it to Kyle.

"Emma, we'll be talking more when we get home," Kyle demanded, shutting her door.

Emma waved to Kyle as she drove off the lot with her new car. As she drove down the road, Emma pulled out her phone to call Micah.

"Hello?" he answered.

"Micah, he said it's not going to be long," Emma sobbed. "I can feel him so close and…I'm scared."

"Do you want me to come over?" he asked.

"I just need some more help working on my powers. I don't think there is much to learn, but I need to make sure that…I don't know…yeah, can you please come over?"

"Yeah, I'll be over in a few minutes." He paused a minute. "Emma…"

"Huh?" She sniffed.

"It'll be okay. I won't let him hurt you," Micah stated.

"Thanks, Micah. I'll see you in a few." Emma ended the call and enjoyed her new car. She didn't know if she would have it for very long, but she was going to enjoy it for as long as possible. She rolled all the windows down, opened the sunroof, and blasted her radio. She felt a little relief from the warm spring air blowing through her hair.

As she pulled into the parking lot, she picked a space that was close to her building and made sure she rolled all of her windows back up. Micah was already waiting for her as she locked her car.

"New ride?" he asked, looking impressed.

"I finally got my own car," she said, smiling widely. Micah gave her a thumbs-up and followed her into the house. "Kyle will be home shortly, he was with me at the dealership. We will probably have to practice in my room."

"Might as well show him," Micah insisted.

"You're probably right. Can I get you anything to drink?" Emma offered as she walked into the kitchen, setting her purse on the table.

"No, I'm good, thanks. What did you want to work on?"

"This is going to sound dumb, but maybe since Kyle will be here—I put a protection spell on him and I want to make sure that I did it right. Can you help me to make sure?"

"I can try, but I'm not sure what you want me to do."

"I know that you can influence the mind. I made sure to include that in the spell, so it's supposed to help. I want you to try to take over his mind." Emma grabbed a beer out of the fridge and quickly gulped a few sips.

"Emma, so we're going to talk now!" Kyle shouted as he walked into the house. "Oh, hey, man, how's it going?" he asked Micah. Micah held out his hand and pulled him in. He began to try to get inside Kyle's head. "Micah, you staring at me like that…it kinda creeps me out."

"Well, you did it right." Micah chuckled.

"Did what right?" Kyle asked, confused, taking a few steps away from Micah. "Emma?"

"Let's sit down," Emma suggested as she handed a new beer to Kyle. "So, my dad is telling me that the time has come." She sighed.

"The time has come? Like he's coming over tonight?" Kyle panicked.

"I don't know. It could be in the next few minutes or he could be messing with my head and it's never gonna happen. I really don't know, but I put a protection spell over you this morning before we left. I just wanted to make sure that it was done right, so I had Micah try to use his powers on you."

"Oh, okay, I thought that our time at the bar was fun, but for a second there, Micah, I thought you read the whole night out wrong." Kyle sighed with relief.

"Wait, what?" Micah asked, throwing his hands in the air.

Emma began to laugh hysterically. The look on both of their faces at the misunderstanding was priceless. She was actually pretty happy that they were taking some of the bad thoughts off her mind. "Kyle, will you make your awesome spaghetti? Micah, want to stay for dinner?"

Both of them looked at her oddly for changing the subject, but nodded at her. Kyle got to work on dinner and Emma and Micah made their way into the living room. She wanted to work on more of her powers, but knew that she was never really going to be strong enough. She knew she had more powers, and she could only hope she'd be ready to use them. So rather than worrying anymore, she and Micah took a seat on the couch. Right now, she just wanted to snuggle into him and feel safe, but her phone rang and as she picked it up she saw Mason's number.

***

Emma quickly ran to her room before the last ring. While sitting next to Micah, she actually contemplated pressing *ignore*. She couldn't do that to Mason though.

"Hi!" she answered.

"I realized it was only Tuesday and I'm begging for Friday to hurry and get here," he said, laughing.

"I know! Only three more days. How's practice?" Emma sat down on her bed and continuously checked her door to make sure that Micah didn't just walk in.

"Brutal. I'm off about nine, so I was thinking we could do a late dessert. Thoughts?"

"Oh man, that is kind of late. I've been sleeping a lot less the last few days, so I might call it an early night."

"Right. Maybe you should tell them blokes to stop coming around," he joked.

Kyle opened her door and poked his head in. "Dinner is ready," he whispered. She nodded and mouthed "One sec."

"Well, I made Kyle cook dinner tonight, so I'm going to go stuff my face and head to bed. Are you free around noon tomorrow? Maybe we can go have some lunch."

"Can do, love. Sleep well, okay?"

"Bye, Mason." She hung her phone up and threw herself back onto her bed. How could two guys make her feel this way? When she was with one she was always thinking about the other. She sighed as she pushed herself off the bed and sulked to the dining room. Micah was fixing her a plate of noodles while Kyle was pouring her a glass of wine. "Okay, seriously who are you two?" She chuckled.

The three of them sat around the dining room table and enjoyed the noodles and wine.

"Em, do you remember much of your childhood?" Micah asked curiously.

"I can remember some things, why?" she asked, taking a sip of her wine.

"I just wanted to see if you remember much about your dad. I know your mom put a spell on you to forget, but I wasn't sure if you know anything about it."

Kyle watched curiously as they talked.

"I…I have dreams. I had a dream about me drawing him a picture and then he…" Emma paused, trying to recall the moment. "He wasn't, or I guess hadn't been himself for a little while." Emma stopped because she suddenly was remembering the entire day—moments of before the whole incident started to cloud her mind. "He had stopped talking to my mom and me for about a month. My mom and he would fight after she would put me to bed. She'd storm down to the basement and I could hear everything. She'd tell him that he needed to seek help."

"You're remembering, aren't you?" Micah asked, leaning toward her and grabbing her hand.

"Yeah," she whispered. "Ying was my mom's friend. Wow, I can see her," Emma stated, closing her eyes. "She worked with my mom at the bookstore and would help my mom out when my dad was locking himself in the basement."

"She told me that she adored you as a child."

"Why was she helping my dad?" Emma asked, confused.

"She wasn't really ever helping him. She never wanted to see you hurt. Neither of us did."

"I'm so confused right now," Kyle chimed in.

Emma chuckled. "Sorry, Ky. I'm just remembering things from my past. My mom tried to erase my mind of all that had happened. My dad tried to actually hurt me when I was younger and wasn't able to succeed then either."

"That means if he couldn't then, he won't be able to now," Micah reassured her. Emma smiled and leaned back in her chair.

"That's right, Em. If I have to I'll step in." Kyle laughed.

"Let me know how that works out for you, Kyle. He's only out for me."

"Well, if you made me some sort of super human and I can even deflect Superman here and his mind reading, I can take him."

"I wish it were that simple, but my dad is powerful. I don't really understand how I'm stronger than him if he can do all these things," Emma stated. She was starting to feel a little confused.

"It's not that you're stronger—it's that you have more abilities. Ones that you have yet to learn. You'll get there one day, I promise." Micah smiled and winked at her.

"If I live to learn them," Emma snapped.

"We're not going to let anything happen to you!" Kyle stated, standing up, raising his glass. "Even if I get knocked on my ass by some hocus pocus bullshit, I will make sure that you stay safe."

"Kyle, I think your tolerance for alcohol is fading," Micah joked. Emma snickered into her glass.

"Dude's got jokes now?" Kyle laughed.

Emma poured each of them another glass of wine. If she could keep this very moment for the rest of her life, she would. It was incredible moments like this that made her life anything but ordinary.

Micah stuck around for another couple of hours and made sure that everything seemed secure around the place. Emma, unbeknownst to Micah, placed a secure spell on him. She couldn't bear losing him, even if she wasn't meant to be with him.

After Micah left, she lay on her bed and tried to only fill her thoughts with happy memories of her and her mom and Kyle, yet every time she closed her eyes she only saw her dad's cold eyes staring down at her.

Chapter Fifteen

"You know, no matter what you do you won't be able to protect everyone," he said snidely.

"Why can't you just leave with the powers you have? I wouldn't ever try to take yours or interfere with anything that you do!" Emma begged.

"Because, Emma, I don't want to ever have that feeling of being less powerful than my daughter. I don't like that idea. Just come to me and give them to me. It'll be quick and painless."

"I...I can't leave everyone. I...I don't want to die!" Emma sobbed.

"You will either way. I'm sure you'll be missed. Your mother, she adores you, but can't keep you hidden forever. Things will be hard on people for a while, but people move on. They forget. Just give up."

"No," she whispered.

"I'm sorry, what did you say?" Sebastian asked.

"No!" Emma screamed, "I will not just give up. I will kill you if I have to, but this will be over and it won't be me dying!"

"We'll see."

***

Emma sat up in bed, breathing heavily. The dreams the last couple of nights had been intense. She felt like shit. Even after she had taken a long hot shower and tried to clear her head, she couldn't get her dad's face out of her dreams.

"Your turn to be hungover?" Kyle joked, handing her a mug full of coffee.

"Not hungover. Just a horrible dream that I can't snap myself out of." She sniffed.

"Well, here's some news to cheer you up. Karen texted me last night and said she'll be back in town this weekend and would love for all of us to get together," Kyle said cheerily.

"Oh, that is good news. See, she still likes you!" Emma nudged his arm.

"Yeah, I guess when it comes to chick stuff, maybe I should listen to you."

"Damn straight, I'm always right!" Emma tried to keep a straight face, but Kyle began to laugh and she couldn't hold it back. "Oh, so tomorrow night Mason has a game. Wanna go?"

"Don't you wanna take your other boyfriend?" Kyle joked.

"What?" Emma asked, confused. *"Other* boyfriend?"

"Yeah, you and Micah seem to be getting cozy again."

"Oh my God! Kyle, I…I didn't mean for it to look like that! Do you think that's what he thinks?"

Emma gasped.

"Not sure what he thinks. I got the friend vibe for a little bit, but when you guys started to pour more wine…it seemed like he was trying to move out of the friend zone and you were letting him. What was it you were doing when he was sitting on the couch?"

"You saw? I was trying to cast the spell on him."

"It was kinda creepy to see you standing behind him, acting like you were going to rub him. Hopefully he didn't see your reflection in the TV and think you secretly wanted to make out with him." Kyle chuckled as he picked up his bag.

"Oh shit!" Emma screeched embarrassedly.

"Dude, your face is so red! Speaking of red, wanna drive? Better yet, let me drive your car," he insisted, holding his hand out for her keys.

"Get your own new car! If you want in my car, I'm driving." She laughed. Kyle huffed as he followed her down the stairs. She was going to enjoy this new car as much as possible. She figured once she was gone, Kyle could then enjoy it. Emma wanted to try and be happy as long as she could.

***

Emma felt in a daze the rest of the day. Paula had to constantly repeat herself. Emma apologized several times, but it didn't get better. After lunch, Emma then realized Paula had gone back to her desk.

"Hey," Emma said quietly, walking into Paula's office.

143

"Hi."

"I'm really sorry about today. I've been having a really off day and I didn't mean to seem like I was ignoring you. Make it up to you? Dinner and drinks after work? I'll bring Kyle."

Paula smirked. "I'd like that."

"Okay, good. Now come back up front so I can have your smiling face cheer me up," Emma insisted.

Paula grabbed her pile of paperwork and followed Emma back to the front. "Oh, Emma, I don't know if I told you. Your mom called while you went outside to breathe. She told me to tell you that she and her boyfriend are fine and they will call you when they get back."

Emma looked at her, puzzled. "Did they say where they went?"

"I'm sorry, she didn't. She was kind of in a hurry and…I should've gotten you."

"No, don't be. You didn't know." Emma smiled. "I'll just try her phone again." Emma wished that she had Connor's number to try to reach them that way.

Emma tried to keep her mind clear for at least the rest of the day. She couldn't help but wonder where her mom was. It wasn't like her to not tell her where she was going or fill her in on some marvelous trip. She really began to worry. Emma needed a lot of drinks tonight. She walked over to Kyle's desk and sat down next to him. "Drinks and dinner tonight. Paula, you, me," she informed him.

"All right. What's the occasion?"

"I need alcohol and I invited Paula to go out."

"Sounds good. Well, you ready to go, then?" Kyle asked, checking the time. It was already near five.

"Sure. Let me go grab my things." Emma excitedly rushed back over to the desk and tapped Paula on the shoulder. She was on the phone and jotted down on a slip of paper that she would be a few minutes and would meet them at a place.

Emma nodded and scribbled the name of the Mexican restaurant and gave her a thumbs-up. Paula nodded and waved to Kyle and Emma as they walked out the door.

***

While Kyle and Emma waited to be seated, Emma felt like something was wrong. She looked around the restaurant. Every other man in the place appeared to look like her dad, until she took a second look. Either she was going crazy or he was able to play mind games on her.

"Em, are you okay?" Kyle asked. He could tell she was in full panic mode.

"Ye...no. I need to get some air," she said, running outside. She started to feel like everywhere she went she was living in fear. As she took several breaths in, Paula walked around the corner.

"Hey! Sorry it took me so long. Did you guys get a table?" Paula asked, walking up to Emma. "Are you okay?"

"Yeah, just...no, we didn't get a table yet. Kyle is waiting inside." Emma sighed. She started to calm down. "Let's go inside and drink heavily,"

Emma joked.

Paula followed Emma in and found Kyle sitting at one of the booths. He looked at Emma, concerned, but she waved him off. She was going to try to ignore everything that was going on today.

The three of them ended up making it a great night. After three margaritas, Emma was finally feeling the relief of not having to worry about the rest of the night. She felt bad for having to drink excessively in front of her new co-worker, but Paula was too interested in Kyle, who shamelessly flirted with her the entire night.

"I. Am. Drunk," Emma slurred as she took a sip from her glass.

"I wish I could say that I even had a buzz." Paula sighed. "But, I only had the one."

"Well, ladies, then let's get you home. Paula, can I give you a lift?" Kyle asked, smiling.

"Tell him no, it's a trick question. He's a pervert." Emma snickered. She turned to Kyle and said, "You can give her a *car* ride home."

Paula laughed. "I'm fine. I live just five minutes away from here. Thank you, though." Emma could tell she was blushing.

"All right, well, if you ever want a ride," he paused, winking, "just call me."

"Seriously, dude? Now you sound creepy. Paula, I'm so sorry. He must be off his game tonight, or at least I hope so, cause…gross!" Emma grimaced. Paula was laughing hysterically as they all walked to the parking lot.

"Thanks, guys. See you tomorrow!" Paula shouted, walking to her car.

Kyle helped Emma into the passenger seat. "What is wrong with me?" He sighed.

"I don't know! Maybe you *need* to get laid. That was just weird."

"Well, just two more days. I'm gonna have to have the place to myself on Friday, okay? Can you go stay with Micah or Mason?"

"Why'd you have to bring up Micah?" Emma snapped.

"Sorry," he replied solemnly.

"It's fine. I'll go to Mason's. Are you going with me tomorrow night?" Emma quickly changed the subject.

"Yeah, it'll be my first soccer game. So I'm kinda excited." Kyle started up Emma's Jeep. "Dude, this thing has some power in it. I'm glad I got you drunk, so I could drive," he joked.

"Ass." Emma chuckled.

"Are you gonna get that?" Kyle asked, hearing her phone vibrate in the cup holder on the console.

"Oh, I thought it was yours." Emma picked up her phone; it was a number that she was finally excited to answer. "Hi, Mason!" she said excitedly.

"Hi, love. Where you at?" he asked.

"On my way home," she answered skeptically. "Why?"

"I'm actually waiting outside your apartment. Practice ended a bit early and I can't wait to see you."

Emma sighed. "All right, should be there in a few minutes." She couldn't want to see him either. Kyle looked at her with a knowing look and nudged her elbow a few times. "Oh stop," she giggled.

"Someone is in L-O-V-E!" he joked.

"Kyle, I'm not in love. I just enjoy being around him."

"Can I ask a serious question before we get home?"

"Sure," she breathed.

"Were you in love with Micah?"

Emma didn't know how to even answer that. She sat there and thought for a moment. "Kyle, I honestly don't know if I was or not."

"I call bullshit!" he exclaimed.

"How so?" she asked in shock.

"Emma, I saw the way you were with him when you were together, and when he left you spent several days in your room moping! Then last night…Emma, the way you two look at each other is the look of someone who is still in love with someone. When I see you with Mason, don't get me wrong, I can tell you like him and all, but it's not the same look you give Micah."

"Of course it's not the same look! They are totally different people!" Emma explained.

"No, this is something different. I can tell with you, Em. I didn't even get the look."

"'Cause you're like a brother!" Emma felt like she was getting way too defensive for this conversation. "Look, I really fell for Micah, yes, but…"

"Em, just remember if Micah is going to be around, things with Mason are going to get more difficult."

Emma nodded as they pulled into the parking lot. Mason was waiting on the outside stairs. She felt a sense of guilt hit her as she walked closer to him. Was Micah really the one she wanted to be with? Was Mason just filling the space for now? She had so much going through her head and the alcohol wasn't helping the situation.

Emma led Mason upstairs and directly to her bedroom. She ran and jumped onto her bed as Mason watched her in amusement. She needed to talk to him seriously and it was now or never. Liquid courage was kicking in.

"Mason, I hate to ask this, but can we talk?" Emma felt her stomach twist into knots and could only imagine what must be going through his mind.

"Are you okay?" he asked, sitting next to her on the bed.

"I just…do you think that we…do you like where this is going? Between us, that is."

"Uh, yeah? Where's this coming from?" he asked nervously.

"I don't know. A lot of my past is coming back into my life recently and I just want to make sure that you like me enough to hang around."

Mason grabbed Emma's hand and looked deep into her eyes. "The past never truly disappears, Emma. I definitely want to see where things between us go, but if you are unsure about it…"

"No, I really like you! Sorry that I brought this up." Emma sighed, causing her to let out a yawn.

Mason lay next to her and started to slowly rub her back. "Love, I'm going to head out. You look like you're about to fall asleep and I want you to rest. I'll see you tomorrow night at the game and then we have all weekend."

"No, please stay," Emma begged. "I think I sleep better with you here."

Mason chuckled. "I'll stay until you fall asleep, okay? We both have early mornings."

Emma nodded and yawned again before she slowly fell asleep.

Chapter Sixteen

Emma woke up with the room completely dark. She realized that at some point Mason had left and turned off the lights in her room. She reached for her phone, which he had plugged into the charger, to check the time. It was nearing midnight. Emma used her powers and flipped the light on. She decided to see if anyone else was awake.

Emma: Are you up?

She couldn't believe she was sending Micah a message.

Micah: Yeah, can't sleep. Why are you up?

How could she explain to Micah that she was up because Kyle had made her think about if she really loved him and if Mason was just temporarily filling the space he had left.

Emma: Can't sleep either. I've been thinking

about my mom. Haven't been able to reach her.

Her phone began to ring and Emma quickly answered it. "Hey."

"What do you mean you haven't been able to reach her?" Micah asked sternly.

"Well, I missed her call at work. I guess she and Connor are on some sort of vacation. It's just that the last time I spoke to her, I kind of snapped at her and I feel like I really should be apologizing to her." Emma sniffed.

"I just talked to Connor," Micah said. "I need to fly back next week and I need him to take me."

"Wait. What? They're back?" Emma asked, confused.

"Em, he didn't mention anything about a vacation. He's been flying this week, and when he's working he can't really take your mom. Sometimes he works for some private parties."

"Micah, you're starting to freak me out. Did he mention anything about my mom?"

"Emma, breathe. I'm sure she's fine. Maybe she was able to fly with him. Call her in the morning. Do you need me to come over?"

"No!" she snapped. "Sorry. I mean, I think I'm just overreacting about everything. I'm going to try to get some sleep." Emma sighed.

"Call me any time, day or night, if you need anything."

Emma nodded even though she knew he couldn't see her. She hung the phone up and snuggled into her pillow. She didn't want to turn the light off. Her mind wouldn't turn off, so she turned on the TV to see if the sound could help her fall asleep.

Show after show, Emma found herself more and more awake. She kept calculating the time in Massachusetts so she could try to call her mom. Emma realized she had stayed awake the rest of the night. It was already five in the morning.

"Emma?" Kyle groggily asked, knocking on her door. "Why is your TV on?"

"Sorry, I didn't realize I turned the volume up," she apologized, reaching for the remote that was under her leg.

"You look like death. You okay?"

"I didn't sleep. At all. I've been up since about midnight. My mind is racing. I think something has happened to my mom and I'm freaking out."

"What's wrong with Grace?" he panicked.

"I don't know. Micah said he just talked to Connor and he hasn't been on vacation, but my mom called and told Paula that they were on vacation. Something feels so wrong about it."

"Emma, I wouldn't worry. Your mom has powers and she can take care of herself. She took care of you all those years. Why don't you call in to work and say you got some sort of food poisoning and I'll cover for you," Kyle suggested.

"That's probably best. Thanks, Kyle." Emma tried to smile, but with the lack of sleep, she had no emotion.

"I'll call you when I'm heading home. If you're still up for it we can go to Mason's game." Kyle scratched his head and started back for his room.

"Can you take someone else? I'm really not in the mood to go. It's going to be really crowded and

I don't think I can handle that amount of people."

"You sure?" Kyle asked hesitantly.

"Yeah, I'm going to call Mason and let him know. I know I just came back this week and I'm probably going to lose my job, but I'll probably take Friday off. I think I jumped into taking on everything too quickly."

Kyle nodded his head in agreement. "I hope this has nothing to do with what I asked you last night."

"Not at all. It did give me something to think about, but it's everything else." Emma rubbed her eyes. "I'm going to try to sleep now. I'll send Phil an email letting him know."

"Call if you need anything. I can come by on lunch," Kyle offered.

"I'll be fine, but thank you." Emma forced a smile.

Kyle left her room, closing her door. Emma dialed her mom's number, hoping to get her to answer. It rang several times, which gave Emma a little more hope, especially since the last few calls went straight to voice mail. This time Emma didn't leave a message, she hung up and rolled over, cuddling into her blankets. She'd forgotten that she needed to send Phil an email, so she grabbed her phone once more and typed out an email. As she pressed *send* a text came through.

Mom: Hi, sweetie. Sorry haven't called. I came down with a cold and have been trying to sleep it off. I love you and promise we'll talk soon.

Emma felt more than relieved to see that

message from her mom, she even began to cry. She laid her phone next to her on the pillow and slowly started to cry herself to sleep. A huge weight had finally been lifted off her shoulders.

***

Emma slept the entire day and through the night. She woke to her alarm beeping from her phone. Emma couldn't believe she slept for twelve hours. Grabbing her phone off her end table, she had several missed texts from Kyle telling her how great the game was, that Mason was just amazing, and that Karen made it back, so he took her. She scrolled through and realized there was a message from Micah.

Emma! You're...

Emma looked at the message several times and didn't understand what he was trying to say. She typed a message, responding.

Micah, is everything okay? I know it's early, but I literally was asleep all day yesterday. I'll explain later. Call me.

Emma pushed herself out of bed and walked down the hall. Kyle's door was wide open and he wasn't around. She figured he spent some time with Karen. Since she told Phil she was missing today, she made some coffee and headed back to her room. Her phone began to vibrate as she sat back on her bed. Mason was already calling.

"Morning, love. I didn't see you at the game. You all right?"

"I'm so sorry, Mason. I wasn't feeling well yesterday, so I stayed home. Can you forgive me?"

"Of course. Are you heading to work today?" he asked curiously.

"You're in luck, I took today off just in case. But am feeling so much better now. How about we spend the day together?"

"I'd love it. Pick you up in a couple hours and we can go enjoy some breakfast, a ride on my motorbike, and then spend the rest of the day locked in my apartment?" He chuckled.

"I can't wait. See you in a bit." Emma hung up and checked her phone. She didn't have a response from Micah. "Calm down, Emma," she whispered to herself. "It is early. He does still have stuff to do for work. He also mentioned he had to get back to New York. Maybe he meant 'you're…wonderful.'" Emma could smell the freshly brewed coffee and fixed herself a cup. The day out with Mason might help her take more things off her mind.

She took her coffee to the couch and cuddled up into the blanket and turned on the news. She'd start getting ready in a few minutes.

As she watched the news, she still had yet to hear from Micah. It made her a little worried that he hadn't replied. She sent him one more message before getting in the shower.

Still no word from you. Actually worried. Call me.

Emma set her mug in the sink and hurried to the bathroom to get ready. She put her phone on the floor next to the tub so she could answer it. It was not like him to not respond. As she stepped in and wet her hair, her phone began to ring. Excited, she threw open the curtain—it was Mason.

"Hey, love, I'll be there in a few. I couldn't wait to see you."

"Oh, I'm just getting in the shower. I'll be done when you get here," she stated.

"No rush, love," he insisted. "I'll see ya in a bit."

"Okay, I'll use my powers to hurry." Emma froze. She couldn't believe she just said that out loud.

"Pardon?" Mason asked.

Emma laughed. "It was a joke, Mason."

"Right. Okay, see you."

Emma hung up the phone and tossed it back on the floor. She smacked her forehead as she used her powers to wash up. She stepped out, reaching for her towel with her powers, and dried herself off as she hurried around picking out some clothes. She'd never been on a motorcycle, so she had no idea what to wear.

She went with a pair of jeans and her knee high boots. Slipping on her boots, she heard a knock at the door. She ran down the hall and saw Mason standing there in jeans and a leather jacket. He looked incredibly sexy.

"Wow, do you have some powers or something? I swear I called only a moment ago and you were in the shower," Mason stated as he walked in through the front door.

"I was just about done with the shower, and I don't mess around when I'm told that I get to ride on a motorcycle," she joked.

"Right," he laughed. "You ready?"

Emma nodded and grabbed her purse. She followed Mason down the stairs and he led her to the parking lot to a beautiful black bike parked next to her Jeep. She clapped her hands excitedly as he handed her a helmet. Before she climbed on, she checked her phone one more time. Nothing. She wasn't going to spend the day worrying.

Chapter Seventeen

Mason took Emma all around the city on his bike. She loved the feeling of freedom on the back of that bike. It felt like she finally had her mind cleared of everything. Mason pulled into a parking lot of a little diner, and her heart stopped when she realized it was the diner that Micah had stopped at when she first met Ying. She hurried off the bike.

"Mason, can you excuse me for a minute? I need to call someone," she said, holding up her phone.

"Sure thing. I'll grab us a table." Mason headed inside the diner and Emma quickly dialed Ying's jewelry shop.

"Hello?" Ying answered.

"Ying! It's Emma."

"Hi, Emma, how are you?" Ying asked happily.

"I'm not so good. I got a message from Micah last night and…well, it didn't really say anything. I've been trying to reach him all morning and I haven't heard from him. It's not like him. You haven't happened to hear from him, have you?" Emma asked worriedly.

"I'm sorry, I haven't, but I planned on meeting him once more before he left. So let me try to call him. Can I call you back?"

"Of course. Thank you, Ying. Ummm…how are you doing?"

"My powers have…" She stopped.

"Ying, I'm very sorry," Emma said solemnly.

"No, please don't be. You saved my life and that is more important than any sort of power."

"Well, I'm glad you're well. If you could let me know, I'll be on my cell."

"Okay. Shouldn't be too long."

Emma hung up with Ying and rushed into the diner. Mason greeted her with a smile. "Everything okay?" he asked.

"I haven't been able to reach Mi…"

"Your ex?" Mason interrupted.

"Yes," she whispered. "He's also a friend, though, Mason. I received a text from him that was very odd and now I'm worried something happened to him." She reached over and grabbed his hand, smiling as Mason nodded, looking over his menu. "I promise that I'm just concerned as a friend," she reassured. Emma's phone rang, startling her. "Hi, Ying?"

"His phone went straight to voice mail. Emma, I'm starting to worry. Look, your father is walking up the sidewalk. Stay safe," she stated, disconnecting the call.

Emma began to panic. "Emma? You okay?" Mason asked worriedly.

"Can we go back to your place for a little while?" she asked, fighting the tears.

Mason nodded, setting the menu back on the table. They gathered their things and headed out the door. Emma knew that it was best to lie low for just a little while until she figured out what was going on. She wished Micah would call her back. Mason sped off down the road toward his apartment.

As she followed him upstairs, she couldn't help a few tears. She quickly wiped them away as he opened the front door to his place. She was in awe of how nice and neat it looked.

"Wow, I love your place," she stated, taking a look around.

"Thanks. It's only temporary. Well, just 'til I can get everything organized. I've been thinking about buying a loft closer to downtown." Mason removed his jacket and placed it on the chair, then slipped his shirt over his head. Emma smiled widely as he came closer to her. He kissed her softly as he pulled her toward his bedroom.

He playfully threw himself on the bed and Emma giggled. Before she could go any further her phone began to ring. It was her mom. She was excited to see someone who would be able to help her.

"Mom! I'm so glad that you're calling!" Emma exclaimed. "Sorry, Mason," she whispered.

"Mom, are you there?" Emma panicked. She could hear some sobs in the background and then a chuckle on the other end.

"Hi, Emma," Karen greeted her on the other end of the phone. Her voice was different.

Emma gasped. "Karen? What are you doing answering my mom's phone?"

"Poor Emma. She wants to talk to her mommy.

Do you know that I never got the chance to meet my mom?" Her voice was so cold it sent chills down Emma's spine.

"Karen, why are you with my mom? What's going on?" Emma panicked, looking at Mason.

"Daddy wants you to come home. I know that you and loverboy are having an amazing day together, but it's time."

"Daddy? What are you talking about? Let me talk to my fucking mom!" Emma shouted. Mason grabbed her hand, looking concerned. Emma shook her head as he mouthed "What's going on?"

"Tsk, tsk. Don't use that kind of language! Just bring your ass home now or she dies. You don't want her to die, do you?"

"Don't you touch her!" Emma paused a moment, only to think of a plan of attack. "I'll come." Emma hung the phone up and tossed it across the room.

"Can you tell me what the hell is going on?" Mason asked, watching her stand up from the bed.

"Mason, it's a long story. I don't even know where to begin with this. Can you just..." Emma looked at him, sitting on the bed. He was going to hate her when all this was said and done. "Mason, there are just a lot of things I never told you about me. I don't know if you're going to handle this well and...can you just come with me?"

"Emma," he started, grabbing her hand, "I really like you. I'm sure anything that you tell me will not run me off."

"You have no idea what you're about to find out."

Mason pushed himself off the bed and grabbed

his t-shirt. Emma picked up her purse off the floor, walking toward the front door of his apartment. She had no idea what to expect when she got home.

Why was Karen with my mom? What the hell was my mom doing in Colorado? And what the fuck was she talking about with 'Daddy'? Emma was so confused by everything. Mason started his motorcycle, handed her a helmet, and she climbed on the back of the bike. The thought of losing her mom began to catch up to her as they pulled away from the curb. Emma could feel the tears blowing off her cheeks as they raced down the road.

***

"Mason, I…I don't know what to expect when we get upstairs. Maybe you should just go home."

"Em, I'm not leaving you. Especially if some psycho bitch has your mum!" He grabbed her hand and they walked up the stairs to the entrance of the building. Emma's heart was racing as they approached the door. She could hear Kyle shouting and Mason pushed her away as he pushed the door open. Emma's worst fear happened. The dream of her mom lying on the floor was coming true. She could see Kyle holding Karen's arms, yelling as her dad stood up from the couch. Micah was sitting next to him. Emma's heart stopped when he finally faced her—his eye was swollen and he had a few bruises on his cheek.

"Hi, Emma," Sebastian said coldly.

"What the hell are you doing here? What's wrong with my mom?" Emma sobbed.

"Emma, I'm fine," Graced whispered faintly.

"Karen, what did you do to her?" Emma shouted.

"Emma, my darling…" Sebastian said, smiling.

"Don't call me that. You lost that privilege a long time ago." Emma scowled at Sebastian, trying to keep her distance from him.

"I'm still your father!" he snapped. "I'd also like to introduce you to your sister, Karen."

"Sister?" Emma screamed, looking at Karen, who was smiling coldly at her. Kyle's jaw dropped and he stepped away from her.

"She's been a wonderful daughter to me. She's been willing to listen to me, unlike another daughter of mine. The only problem, her mother didn't have powers and she didn't get any. So we're here to make sure that she gets your powers."

"Yeah, you're fucking insane!" Emma spat.

"Don't use that tone with me! I can kill you in one move and not give a shit about it, but I need you alive to get your powers. Why don't you take a seat next to your boyfriend on the couch."

"Don't do it, Emma," Mason said, grabbing Emma's arm.

"And who are you?" Sebastian asked.

"I'm…" Mason started, but Emma stepped in front of him.

"None of your business!" Emma turned to Mason. "Please, just go," she whispered. He looked so confused as to what was going on. He shook his head and turned to head back out the door, but it slammed before he could go.

"No, I wouldn't want to have anyone left out of the party. Please, come in. Emma, already moving on from Micah?" Sebastian chuckled. Emma suddenly felt a force pulling her toward Sebastian, and it felt like it was squeezing the air out of her as she got closer to him.

"Sebastian, please," Emma gasped.

"Sebastian! Stop!" Micah shouted, causing him to lose concentration. Emma fell to the floor, trying to catch her breath. She crawled over to her mom, who had a bloody lip and had been crying.

"Are you okay?" Emma whispered. She gave Emma a slight nod before Karen came over and pulled Emma away from Grace.

"Hi, sis," she said snidely. "Why don't you and Mason take a seat on the couch?" She walked over to Kyle. "You too, go take a seat."

"What the hell are you doing, Karen?" he asked.

"Kyle, you were a great lay, but you need to understand that I was just using you to find Emma."

"You really are a crazy bitch," Emma snapped.

"Emma, don't talk about me like that. I'm your baby sister!"

"That's enough, you two," Sebastian stepped in. "Now, Emma, you have a decision. You can willingly give me your powers—which might kill you. Or I can just take them and kill you."

"Wow, that's some choice. What if I take the other option of none of the above?" Emma smirked.

He chuckled. "I kill your mom and then I'll take your powers anyway." Emma's face dropped into a frown. "I see you don't have that smirk anymore. What's your decision?"

Emma stood up and channeled her powers into her fingertips, then pushed Sebastian across the room. Karen came toward Emma and she pushed her down to the ground, making sure that her powers were holding her down. Kyle rushed over to Karen and held her down so Emma could use all her power on Sebastian. Emma felt an electrical shock pushing her down onto the couch. The memory of lifting Micah in the air and him telling her it felt like she was taking his breath away crossed her mind. Emma began to lift Sebastian up in the air, but it was taking a lot of energy out of her.

"Don't break your concentration, Emma," Micah whispered behind her.

"I…I…can't…" Emma felt all her energy drain and she fell back into Micah's arms. Sebastian fell to the floor and quickly pushed himself up.

"I would've thought that you would have more strength than that!" Sebastian evilly laughed. "What else do you *think* you got?"

Looking at Micah, all Emma could picture was him trying to help her with everything. He gave her a wink before turning to Sebastian. "I don't want to hurt you. I don't want that…"

"Then just give up!" Sebastian demanded.

"You didn't let me finish. *But* I will. I'm going to give you the choice to leave now, or I'm going to go really dark. And don't think for one second that I can't."

"Don't threaten me, young lady. I've only *let* you play your little magic on me. You have no idea what you're doing. You need to just give your powers up and let someone who knows *how* to use them have them."

"You think I have no idea what I'm doing?"

Emma asked, feeling like the rest of the room was beginning to get dark. Before she could do anything, Emma saw Sebastian wink at her and take a deep breath in while raising his hands. In one swift move, Sebastian's hands sent a powerful force toward Micah, knocking him to the ground. This time he didn't make any sort of movement. "What did you do to him?" Emma screamed. Mason ran over to Emma and held her back as she tried to run for Micah's lifeless body. She began to cry hysterically, trying to fight her way out of Mason's arms.

"Why would you want to be with him, Emma?" Sebastian asked with an evil smirk. "He's the one who led me to you. He betrayed your trust." He walked over to Micah and nudged him with his shoe.

Emma pulled her arms away from Mason's grip and stared into Sebastian's cold blue eyes, wiping the tears that were falling down her face. He was right; Micah had been the one who helped him find her. He was the one who caused them all to be standing in this room. Her mom was lying on the floor, hurt, and that was all because Micah had helped him. Emma felt worn out by him taking the man she loved away from her. "You're right. He is the reason," she whispered. Emma closed her eyes and took a deep breath in. "But I'm ending this shit right now."

"What?" he snapped. Before he could say or do anything more, Emma channeled all her hatred and emotions and put them all into a ball of energy that shot from her hands toward her father. His eyes widened just before his body was thrown across the room. Emma watched him gasp one last breath of air, before he finally let go. She couldn't believe what she had just done. She had killed the man who was once her father. It was done.

Emma quickly ran to where Micah was lying. "Mom! Can you help me?" she screamed. Emma lifted his head, holding him in her arms.

"Emma…I…" A tear streamed down Grace's cheek. She was so weak. Karen ran to her side and wrapped her arm around her. Whatever Sebastian had done to her, she had forgotten all about it.

"Emma, what about you?" Kyle asked, putting his hand on her shoulder.

"I'm not sure that I can bring someone back. I can heal cuts and bruises, maybe even a broken bone. This is bringing someone back to life!" Emma sobbed.

"You can do it, sweetie," Grace whispered. Emma looked up at Mason. He was standing quietly off to the side, still in awe of all the events that he had witnessed only moments ago. Emma lowered Micah's head to the floor and placed her hands on Micah's chest and closed her eyes. Tears began to stream down her cheeks as she tried to put all her energy into healing him. Emma was so tired and run down from all the power she used against her father. Kyle took a step back as her mom took his place, putting her hand on Emma's arm. "Just breathe, focus on what you are trying to do," she said softly.

"Please, Micah, please," Emma begged. Feeling more power move through her fingertips, she pushed harder into his chest. "God damn it! Wake up!" she shouted. Just then, Micah gasped for air. "Oh my God! I did it!" Emma threw herself down onto Micah, squeezing him tightly.

"Emma! I can't breathe," he gasped.

"Oh shit, I'm sorry," Emma said, pushing herself off of him. "I…I thought I lost you forever."

"Hey, man. I can't believe that I'm actually gonna say this, but I'm glad you're back," Kyle said, kneeling down beside Micah and playfully socking him in the arm.

"Thanks, Kyle." Micah chuckled.

"That and I don't know how the fuck I'd feel about *two* dead bodies in my living room," Kyle joked. Emma punched his arm. "Ow! For a girl, you actually have a mean hook."

"Hey, better watch out. I know how to kill."

"Shit, that's right. Now I'm kinda creeped out that you are just down the hall from me."

"Shut up, Kyle." Emma laughed. "Micah? Are you okay?"

He nodded, grabbing her hand as he sat up. "A little sore, but I'm so glad to see your beautiful face again." He pulled her into him and squeezed her tightly. Emma never wanted to let him go. She heard Mason clear his throat and she quickly stood up and walked over toward him.

"Well, it's been one hell of a day. Who wants a drink?" Kyle asked, standing up. He was trying to clear the room for Emma and Mason to talk. Micah pushed himself off the floor.

"I'll help," Micah mumbled.

Grace grabbed Karen, who looked as if she was waking up from a wild dream, and quickly followed

Micah and Kyle out of the room. There was a lot for everyone to talk about. Emma waited until everyone was gone before she tried to grab Mason's hand, but he pulled away

"Mason, I'm so sorry. I…" Emma started. She really didn't have the words to say.

"Emma, I'm confused right now. I-I…so is that the guy before me?"

Emma nodded. "I know that it's a lot to take in and I hope that I can explain. I really like you."

"That's the thing, Em. You may like me, but it will always be Micah you want to be with," Mason stated, crossing his arms.

"Mason…" Emma sighed. She really was feeling something for him, but knew Micah would have that special place in her heart.

"It's okay. I want you to be happy, Emma." Mason leaned in and kissed her cheek and walked toward the front door. Part of her was really sad— she couldn't believe that she could let him just walk away.

"You okay?" Micah asked, walking up behind her. "I heard the door close. Did Mason leave?"

"Yep. He's gone." Emma turned to face Micah and he rubbed his hands up and down her arms. "Micah, I couldn't stop thinking about you and I really think that you're the only one for me."

"Emma, I really do love you. I don't want anything to ever happen to you." Micah picked her up and pressed his lips hard into hers. Soon, everyone came walking into the room and Micah set her down.

"Sorry, didn't think we were interrupting

anything." Kyle chuckled.

"Nope." Emma blushed, looking over at her father's lifeless body lying on the floor. "Umm…what do we do about him?" Emma asked, pointing toward him.

"I'll handle it," Micah replied as he walked over to him. He stared at him for a moment, shaking his head.

"How?" Emma asked.

"A vanishing spell."

"Can I watch?" Emma excitedly asked.

"Maybe we should leave the room," Kyle suggested, pulling Karen's arm.

"No, it's okay," Micah insisted. "Do you really want to watch him be gone forever?" He turned to face Emma.

"You have no idea." Emma sighed. Micah reached for her hand and pulled her toward him. Emma looked down at Sebastian's face and began to recall the happy times that she once had forgotten, and felt at peace that he was never going to hurt her or anyone else again.

Micah whispered some foreign words as he closed his eyes. Emma was more in awe of Micah working his magic than she was at the slowly fading sight of Sebastian Blackwood. Before she knew it, he was gone. Forever. A single tear rolled down her cheek.

"Emma, I'm really sorry," Micah said, turning toward her.

"It's…Micah, I don't have to live my life in fear anymore. I'm happy that it's done."

"I want another chance with you. One to prove

we are meant to be together." He pulled her closer to him. "I can't lose you again." Lifting her chin, he gently kissed her lips.

"Geez, get a room!" Kyle interrupted.

Emma rolled her eyes, pulling away from Micah, and turned toward Kyle. "Shut up!" Emma laughed and turned back to Micah, pushing her lips hard against his. As she pulled away, Karen was standing off to the side. "Karen…"

"Emma, I'm…I'm gonna go. I really am sorry for anything that I did to you guys," she sobbed.

"Karen, you don't have to say sorry. You were under a very dangerous man's spell. Besides, you're my sister! I'm actually quite excited about this!" Emma said, walking toward her.

"You are? But, I'm nothing special…" Karen sobbed.

"Are you kidding? You're great! Please stay," Emma begged, pulling at her hand.

Karen wiped the tears away and squeezed Emma tightly as she hugged her.

"Hot damn, some sister action," Kyle joked. Everyone turned to face him and gave him a dirty look. "What? Just sayin'!" Karen and Emma shook their heads as Emma's mom smacked his arm.

Emma pushed Karen toward Kyle and watched them slowly hug. They were meant to be and Emma was happy that if Kyle was going to be with anyone it was going to be her sister. Emma wrapped her arms around Micah. He was her everything and she was going to be with him. Forever.

"I love you, Emma Blackwood," he whispered.

"I love you, Micah Oliver." Emma sighed with

relief that everything was finally over.
Or so she hoped.

About the Author

Michelle Escamilla is a married mom of two. She began writing just to pass the time, waiting for one of her favorite authors to release her upcoming book, but soon found a new passion. When she is not writing, she is spending time with her kids, husband or family. She lives in Colorado, where she loves the Mountains during the summer months for hiking and would love to be on a beach during the winter months.

Facebook:
https://www.facebook.com/authormichellee

Twitter:
https://twitter.com/msescamilla

9 781680 584134